S0-AKR-451
FREE HUGS!
FREE HUGS!
FREE HUGS!
FREE HUGS!

FREE HUGS!
FREE HUGS!

DEATH & Sparkles

and the Sacred Golden Cupcake

DEATH & Sparkles

and the Sacred Golden Cupcake

Rob Justus

chronicle books · san francisco

CHAPTER 1

Ewwww!

Oh, great.
A mole
infestation.
Just what
we need.

Aww!
Look at
the cute
babies!

Can we keep them?
Pretty please?

Hmmm . . .
Hrmmm . . .

Pretty, pretty
please?

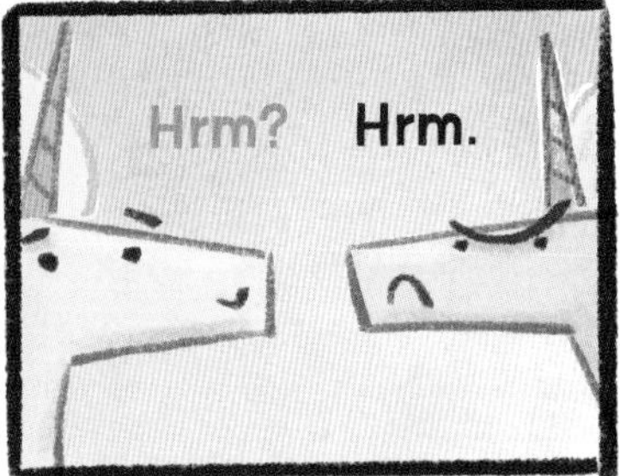
Hrm?
Hrm.

Gah!
Fine!

Yay!

BUT! They stay outside, and they'll have to earn their keep. The moment they're trouble, they are gone. Understand?

Yes, sir! Thank you, Daddy!

Goo-goo-gah.
H'rum!
I better not regret this.

We are going to be best friends forever!
H'rummm.
Haha!
En garde, peasant!
Mmm. Cupcakes!
Yay! Gruel!
Huh.

Hello?

Get up.

Huh?

Where are we going?

It's time for you freeloaders to earn your keep.

Whoa.
H'roa.
You said it, Pink.

This is our most divine sanctuary:
the sacred garden.
It's where uni-colts
become unicorns.

Come inside.

I've never seen anything like this before.

The time for fun and games is over. From now on, you four work and live here. Your jobs are to ensure that everything is in order for the uni-colts' rite-of-passage celebration.

Say goodbye to your easy ride in life.

slam!

Where do
we start?
Do you even
know how
to garden?

What IS
that thing?

CHAPTER 2

AHHH!

SOMETHING'S WRONG
WITH MY HORN!
MY SKIN'S
ALL CREEPY-
CRAWLY!

LOOK!
Gah!

Dude, I'm trying to work.

HURRY! I CAN'T STOP MOVING!

So you're saying that if I order twenty CDs, I can get half off the next one?
Now, that's a deal!

It's like I've got an itch I can't scratch!

Hey!
I'll take this.

Um. This is Death. I've got the runs, so I gotta run!
DUDE!

WHAT'S GOING ON WITH ME?!

Hmmm. Well, I'm no doctor, but it looks like your horn is glowing.

It was its usual pink a minute ago. Now it's like some sort of jazzed-up beacon!

Is it on fire or something?

Nope. It's not that.

Did you eat that expired cupcake we found behind the radiator?

I would never do that.

Well, yeah, of course I did that.

BUT I ate that last week! This JUST started!

I've got this energy coursing through me!

Maybe you're going through a growth spurt?

WAIT! That's it!

Where are you going?

My room!

You mean *my* room.
Well, how come all my stuff is in here, then?
Because you just took over the whole room!
AHA!

What is it?
The only thing my parents left me.
I never knew what it was for until now

click
clunk
creeeeeeeak!
Majestic.

CHAPTER 3

Purple, we've really outdone ourselves this time.

This year we'll finally be able to join the celebration, Brown!

Maybe we'll be able to move out of the shed.

Blue, all our hard work is paying off.

H'rm brp!

That's right! I think we're pals now.

They're always laughing along with us.

I feel like we finally belong now.

Holy sprinkles! They're going to be here any minute.

C'mon, gang! We need to get dressed.

I'm so excited!
Pink, where are my pants?
Mr'umph herm.
You're right. There they are.
F'rm dh-trm!
Absolutely! We are going to blow everyone away with our dance moves!

Maybe we'll get to eat a cupcake!

Better yet, maybe we get to use the Sacred Golden Cupcake!
It's our rite-of-passage party, too.

OH! I think I hear them coming!

Let's go greet our party pals!
Wait for me!

WELCOME, FRIENDS!

Outta the way, mole!

Haha!

Oh! Okay.

STOMP!

STOMP!

STOMP!

STOMP!

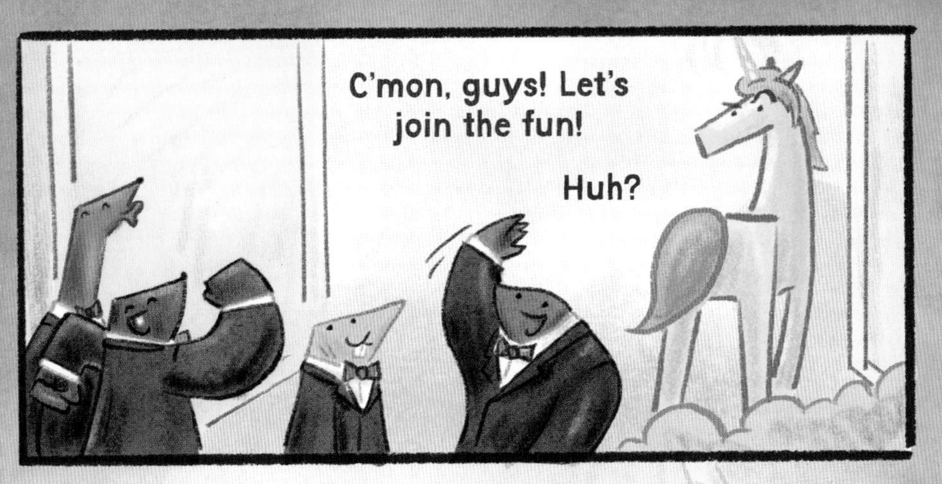

C'mon, guys! Let's join the fun!
Huh?

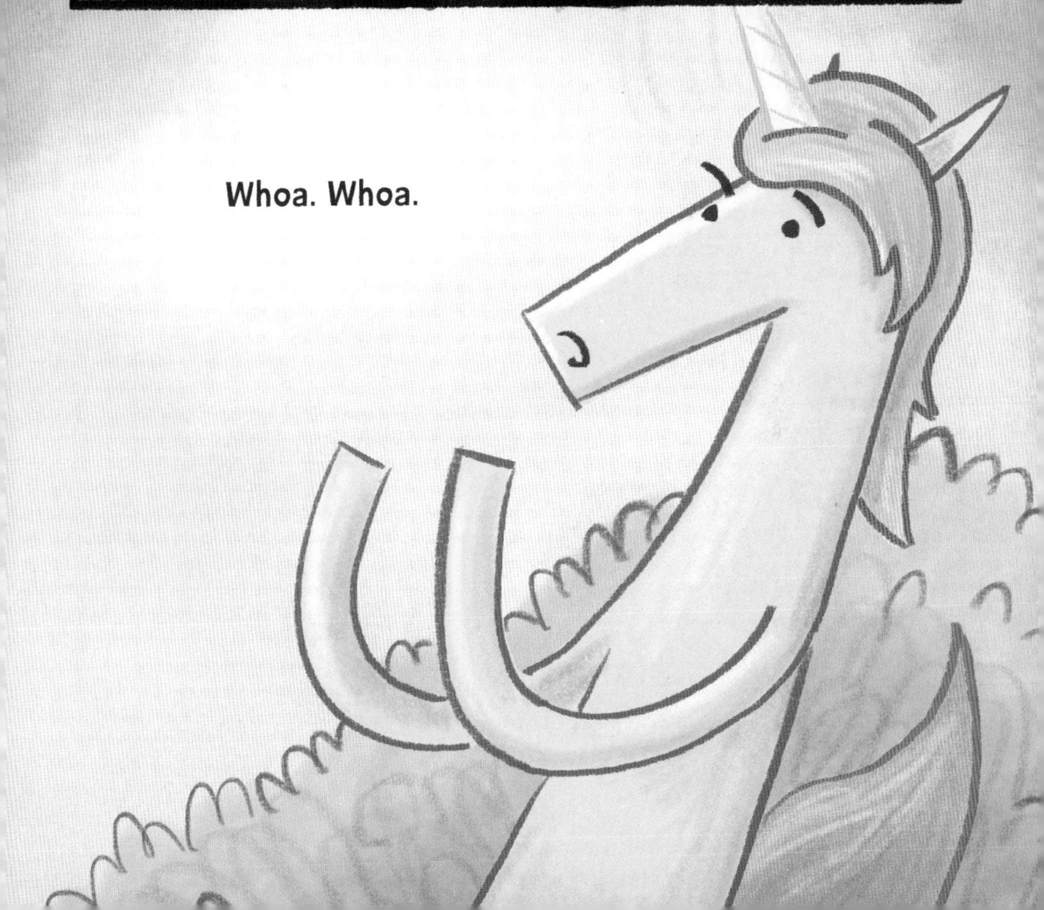

Whoa. Whoa.

Guys, what are
you doing?

Well . . . we're sixteen now.
It's our time to complete
the rite of passage, too.
Just like you!

Why would
you think
that?

I don't know. I thought
we were old friends.

We pretty much grew up
together. Sure, you got to
live in a big, comfy mansion,
while we lived in an old barn.
We're pretty much
honorary unicorns.

Psshhhhh!

You really think we're friends???

Well . . . yeah!

Aw, Purple. I mean, we always had a great time together, but . . .
You're my *pets*. Not my friends.

Plus, this is a dance party. Everyone knows moles can't dance.

Unicorns only. Always and forever.

sniff

We can dance.

Wow! They're really having a blast in there.
H'orm doop pun!
D'uhh . . . doop-duh-duh.
You're right, Pink. I think they're making fun of us.
HA! HA! HA!
HA! HA! HA! Stupid moles!
You okay, Purple?

WHY??

Every year, we go out of our way to make *their* party something extra special.

Is it not our rite of passage, too? Is it too much to make *us* feel special???

ptoie

splat!

We'll show them!

They're going to regret not wanting to be our friends.
We're going to hit them where it hurts . . .

Right in the cupcakes!

CHAPTER 4

It's breathtaking.

What a fancy letter!

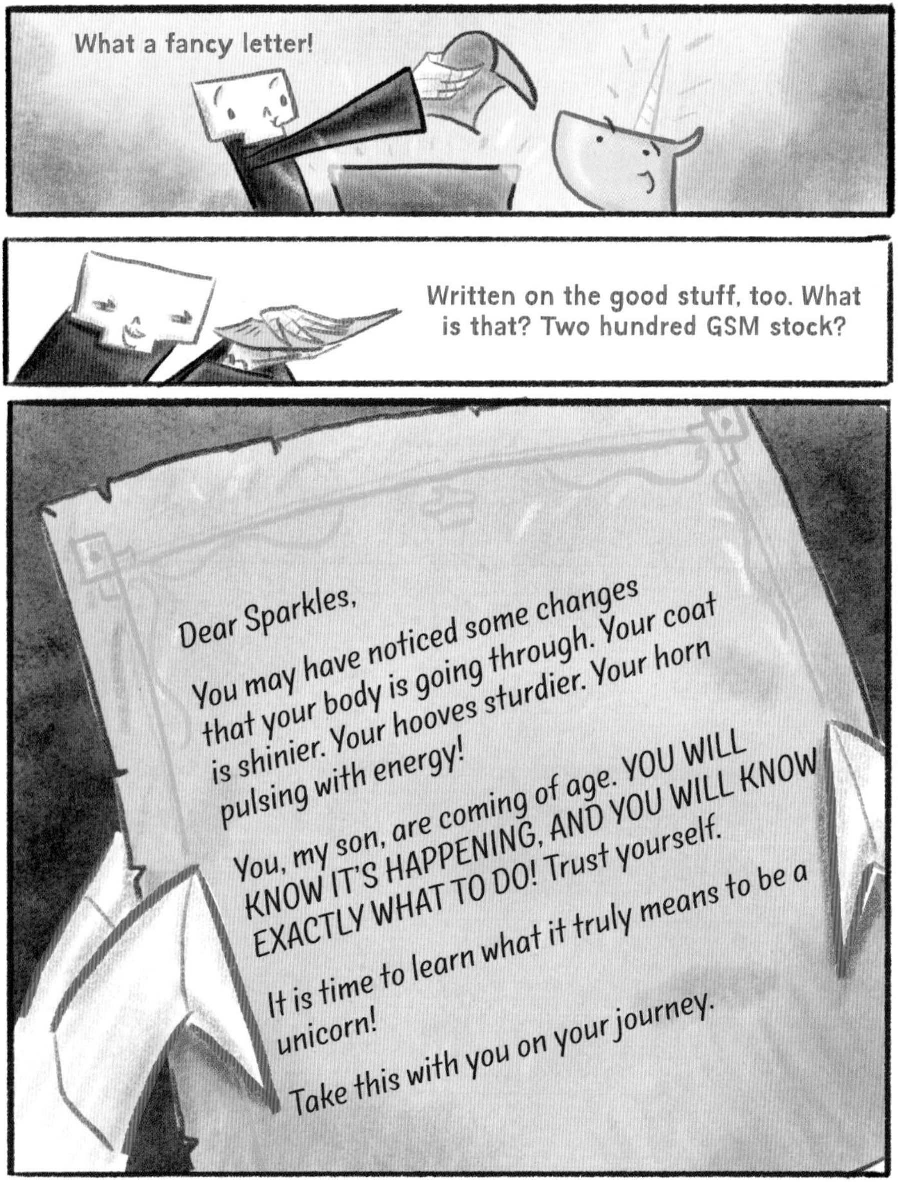

Written on the good stuff, too. What is that? Two hundred GSM stock?

Dear Sparkles,

You may have noticed some changes that your body is going through. Your coat is shinier. Your hooves sturdier. Your horn pulsing with energy!

You, my son, are coming of age. YOU WILL KNOW IT'S HAPPENING, AND YOU WILL KNOW EXACTLY WHAT TO DO! Trust yourself.

It is time to learn what it truly means to be a unicorn!

Take this with you on your journey.

Okay. So what journey is this letter taking? We gotta mail it or something?
Not the letter. The other thing in the box.

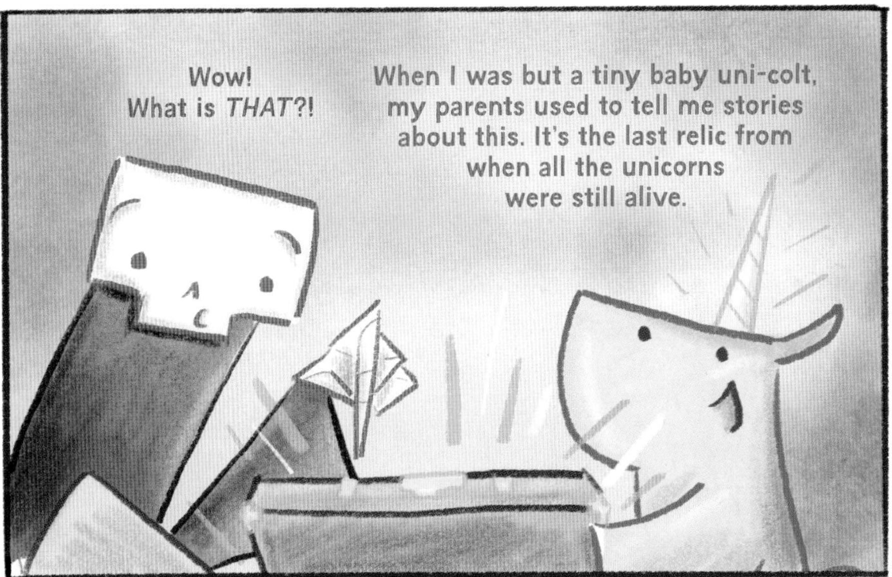
Wow! What is *THAT*?!
When I was but a tiny baby uni-colt, my parents used to tell me stories about this. It's the last relic from when all the unicorns were still alive.

It's my supersweet . . .

Okay. So, what now?
The letter says you'd
know what to do?

CUPCAKE
BLING!

Ooooooh, fancy!

Oh, I know
what we have
to do . . .

We have to DANCE!!!

Wait, what? Dance?

Are you sure we're not supposed to just play video games?

YOU can play video games. *I* have to dance.

Karaoke?

Dancing.

Okay,
I'll set up
living

No living room dance party tonight, pal

I'm not sure where my horn will take us, but I need to bring this sweet bling there and dance my little unicorn heart out. Hopefully I'll learn about my ancestors. I can only assume they were super cool like me. Must be genetic.

So get your best rags on!
And maybe wear this, this, and this.

Tonight we're going

OUT!

Clubbing? I think
I'd rather work.

CHAPTER 5

The Sacred Golden Cupcake.

Do you really think we should steal this?
It's not stealing. We're just playing a big prank! Besides, after all we've done for those jerk 'corns, how dare they think they're better than us. How dare they laugh in our faces after all the work we do for them!
Now we'll see how funny it is when they realize their Sacred Golden Cupcake is gone!

I brought masks
so no one knows
who we are.

I'm not wearing a mask!

Those ain't fooling
anyone.
H'rah!

Fine, then.
You can wear
this disguise.

This is so stupid.

Ah, much
better!

Let's get on with it.

Nice and quiet now.
H'rokee.
Nothing to see here.
rustle
shuffle shuffle
These glasses are SO thick.
I can't see a thing!

POK!
CLANG!
CRINK!

Shhh!

Don't
shush me!

Oof!
Hey!
squish
Ouch!
Hr'ch!
WAAAAAH!

THUD!

THAT'S IT! I'M
TAKING THESE OFF!

Not sure you
should do that.

Whoa.

TWEEEEEEEEEET!
gulp

STOP RIGHT THERE!!!

Are you trying to steal our most sacred and magical artifact? Gifted to
by the great purple protector. The
ragon that has blessed us with vast
ortune and true knowledge of the
niverse and all the secrets that
with it. The one true mystic
that us noble unicorns
source for which prov
supre power.
helps oung
int

unicorns you see before you. Not to mention that it gifts us with magical bounty that grows our spirits, lifts us above eve er b this so that
we ca ple tures to a better life. Where
wou tho lessed superior beings?
T n ke some lowly lizards?

SHEESH!
Get on with it, pal.

Unmask yourselves!
Really?! You can't tell who we are?
Quit your mind games, stranger!
sniff
sigh

GASP!
No. It can't be. Never in a million-bajillion years would I have thought you guys would do this.

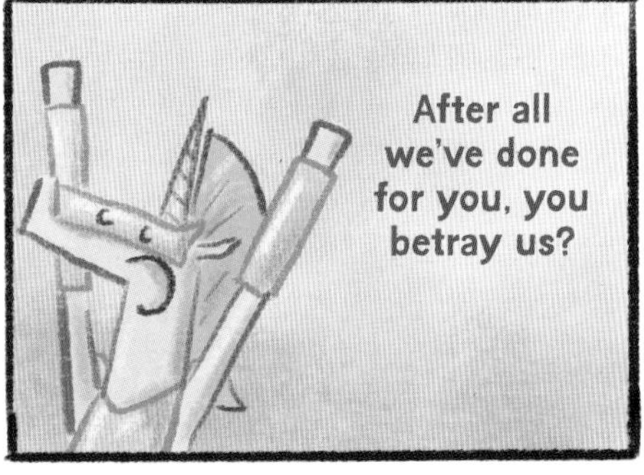
After all we've done for you, you betray us?

Why would you do such a thing?

Ptoie!
We don't answer to you smug fools anymore!

GASP!

You 'corns are too busy eating cupcakes to realize you're all jerks!

We'll see about
that, traitors!

CHAPTER 6

Everyone
is laughing
at us.

ENTER
DANCE
So what?

Those losers wouldn't know style if it hit them right in the face!
Plus, you're Death! Anyone gives you trouble, just touch them and they'll be gone. Dead. Kaput!

SMACK!

TH'NK!
beep! beep! beep!

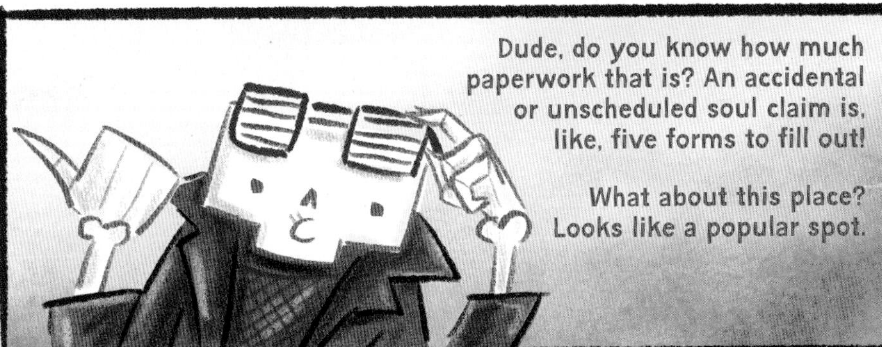
Dude, do you know how much paperwork that is? An accidental or unscheduled soul claim is, like, five forms to fill out!
What about this place? Looks like a popular spot.

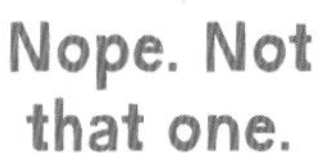
Nope. Not
that one.

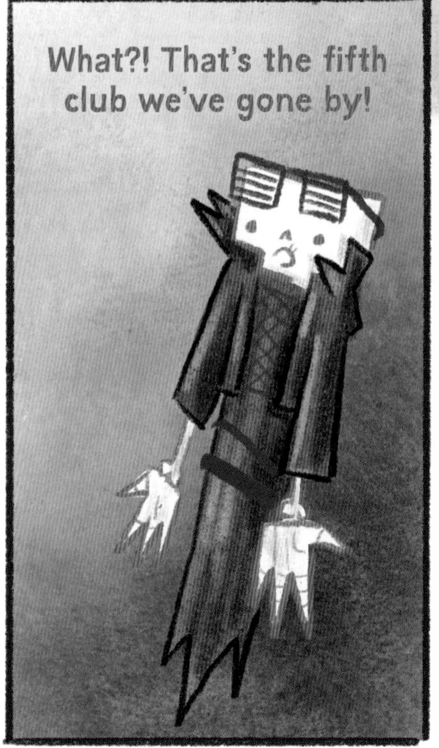
What?! That's the fifth
club we've gone by!

LE CLUB
DANCE
And that one
specifically says
DANCE CLUB!

It's not just any dance club we're looking for.

I'm being drawn somewhere. Someplace *fantastic*.

Fine. Whatever. You better show me some serious moves when we get there.

You know I'm not a good dancer. That's *your* thing. I don't even have feet.

You just need to feel the rhythm.

C'mon, my horn is
telling me it's this way.

Are we there yet?

Nope.

Now?

Nope.

NOW?
Nope.

NOW?!
Nope.

Nope.

Nope.

whoosh!
Nope.

Can you STOP swinging that thing around?

It helps me concentrate!

Oy! Your weird pony just smashed my ride!

D'NK!

D'NK!

Here, take this!
SPARKLES, LET'S GET OUT OF HERE!
whistle whistle
Huh?
Just tell me where to go—fast!
WHOA!

Go left!

Turn right!

Through here!
scccr'tch!
My shirt!

Up here!

JUMP!
AHH!

Oof!
Spin!

Down here!
snap!
D'ah!

Keep going!

WHEEEEEeee!
AHHHHHHH!

CRASH!
Time to lie down.
shuffle
shuffle
Woo-hoo!
That was fun!

Can we go home now?
No way! We're close. I can feel it.

I'm getting that feeling.

FOLLOW ME!

You've got to be kidding me.

TA-DA!
This is the spot! Right down here.
sigh

A pipe?? There's no
dancing in a pipe!

What's with all
the mushrooms
growing around it?

Doesn't
matter.

My horn is saying
we're in the right place.
Look
at it!

My horn's drawing me here. We need to drop down into it.
Seems pretty random . . .

. . . but oddly familiar.
For some reason, it reminds me of mustached plumbers.

It does, doesn't it?

We don't even know where it goes?

It must be one of those super-secret underground clubs.

So secret people die trying to find it! Not worth the paperwork!

It looks like it leads to sewage.

Correction. It leads to adventure.

I liked our first adventure better. This one seems like a lot more work.

It'd be easier if you just went with the flow.

I'll just dance my way through this epic unicorn mystery all by myself.

I'm going where the
beats are fresh and the
moves are slick!

No, thank you. You've
dragged me all over town.
I draw the line at
random green pipes!
So you're on
your own, pal!
Oh, yeah?

You won't need these then.

HEY!

H'rumph! Fine, then.

Have fun by yourself.

Go into the unknown by yourself.

(What was that sound?)

clang!

bang! bang!

I'll stay here by my—uh—self . . .

REOOWR!

AHHHHHH!

CRASH!

bloop
bloop
bleep
Wait for me!

CHAPTER 7

THUNK!
THUNK!
THUNK!

GUILTY!

By way of the magical Sacred Golden Cupcake, you four are to be cursed to the darkness of the underground for the rest of eternity, never to return to our bright and beautiful unicorn kingdom.

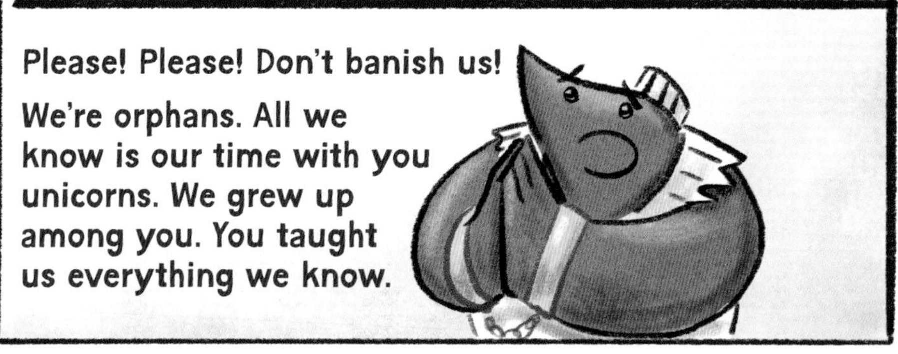

Please! Please! Don't banish us!
We're orphans. All we know is our time with you unicorns. We grew up among you. You taught us everything we know.

It's clear we made a mistake in letting you live among us. You betrayed our trust. This kingdom is for unicorns only.

Always and forever.

It was just a
harmless prank.

We'll do anything.
We'll work in the
cupcake factories.
Anything!

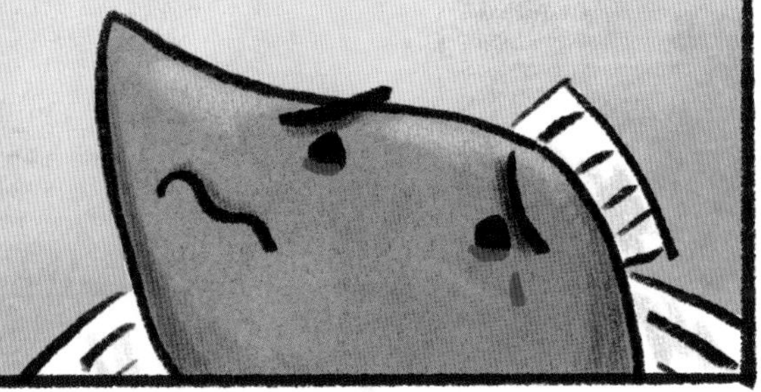

Just not the
darkness.

Working in the cupcake factory would be a paradise for what you've done.

You defiled the sacred garden.
You tried to take our most precious artifact.
You betrayed our trust!
We took you in. We gave you a place to stay. We gave you a purpose.

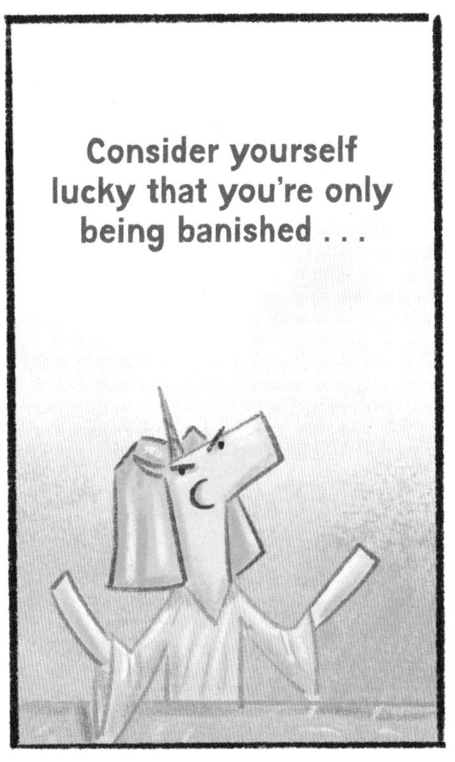
Consider yourself
lucky that you're only
being banished . . .

And not being sent
to the great dragon!

May your time cursed in the dank
and desolate underground give you
pause for all that you've done.

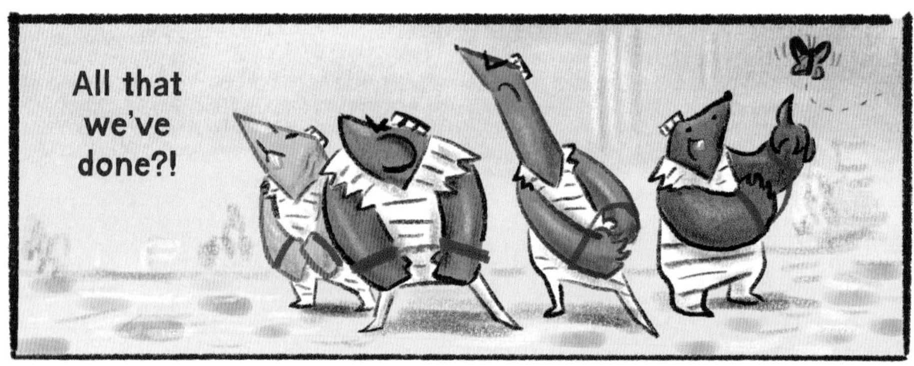
All that we've done?!

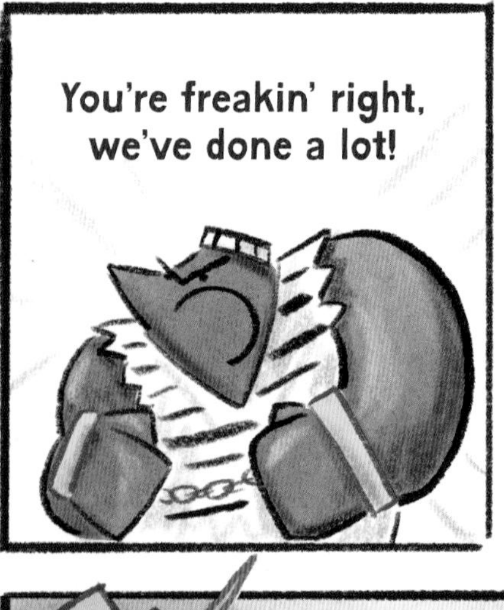
You're freakin' right, we've done a lot!

We cared for your sacred garden. Made it beautiful for your most sacred day. For your big party!

Get them out of here! Commence the spell!

Ooooommmm . . .

Almighty Cupcake.

All we wanted
was to be part of
the fun!

May your sugary magical goodness protect us from these traitors.

To be accepted.

To be friends.

May your sweet frosting seal the traitors below for all eternity!

But you just looked down your snouts at us.

You only saw us as "the help."

Who will help you unicorns now?

YOU HAVEN'T SEEN THE LAST OF US!

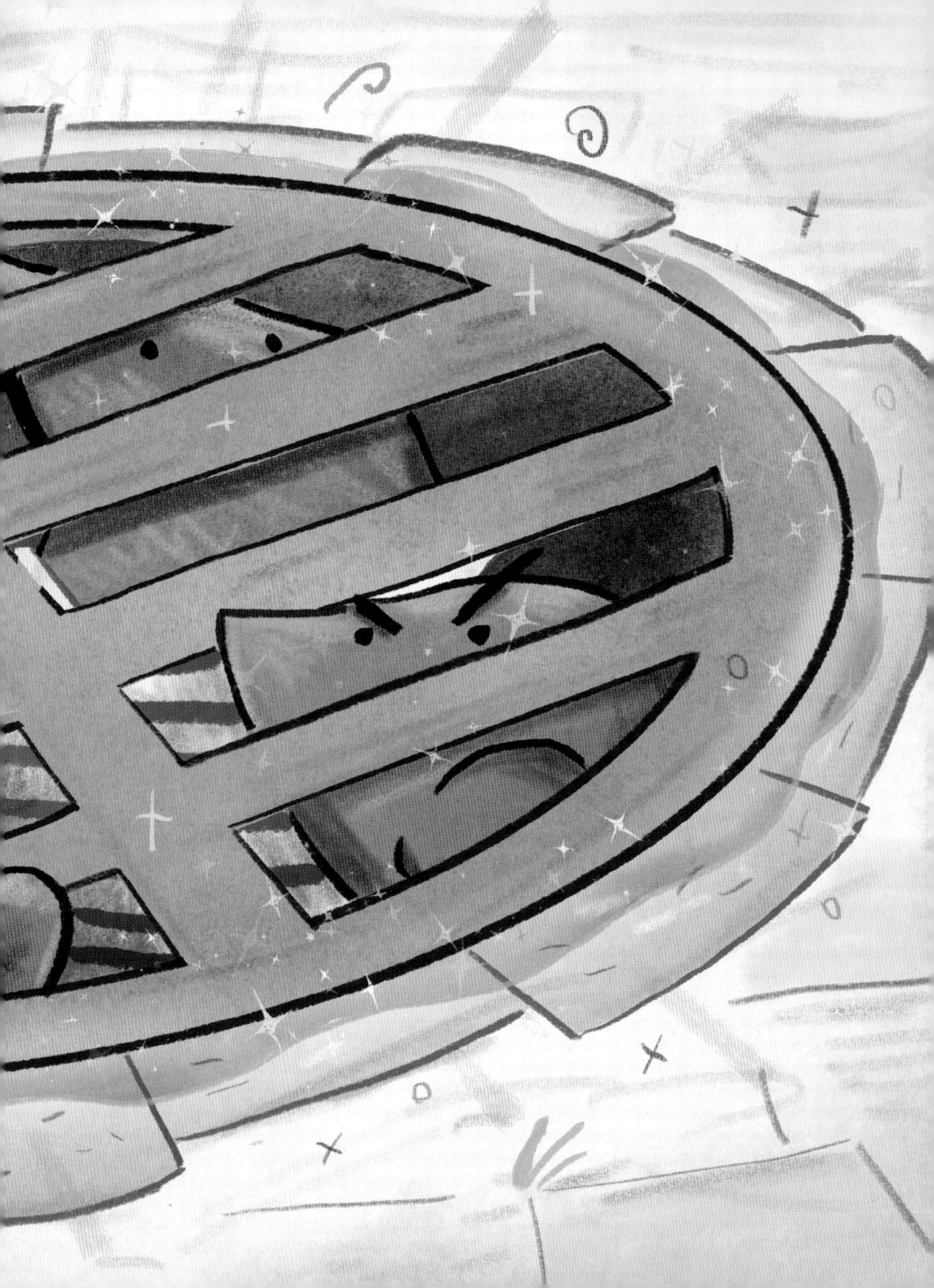

CHAPTER 8

AHHH!

AHHH!

bloop
bloop
bleep
crash!

How'd you
catch up to me?

Good question.
Maybe I'm just
heavier than you?

You are literally
rags and bones.

Whoa. Sparkles, your horn is really sparkling now! Like, mega glitter.

Holy cupcakes, it is!

Bleh! I think I've got your glitter in my mouth.

Whoa.

That's where we need to go.

Is that
really a
dance club??
I think so. That's
where my horn is
pulling me.

What's it
surrounded by?

Is that
a maze?

It better not be
another obstacle
course. Amirite?

Dude, a maze IS
basically an
obstacle course.

Let's go check it out!

Wow!
This is epic!

Yeah, I guess you were right. I never knew they meant these hip clubs were LITERALLY underground.

I'm always right. You just gotta believe in the power of the horn, bay-bay!

Still, something seems fishy.

Wow! Look at that statue!
Look at the fine craftsmanship! My ancestors must've made this exquisite piece!
Let's get a selfie in front of it.

Woo-hoo!
Golden winged
cupcake selfie!

ker'chunk!

What was that?
Huh. That stone sank
when I stepped on—

AH!

k'clank!

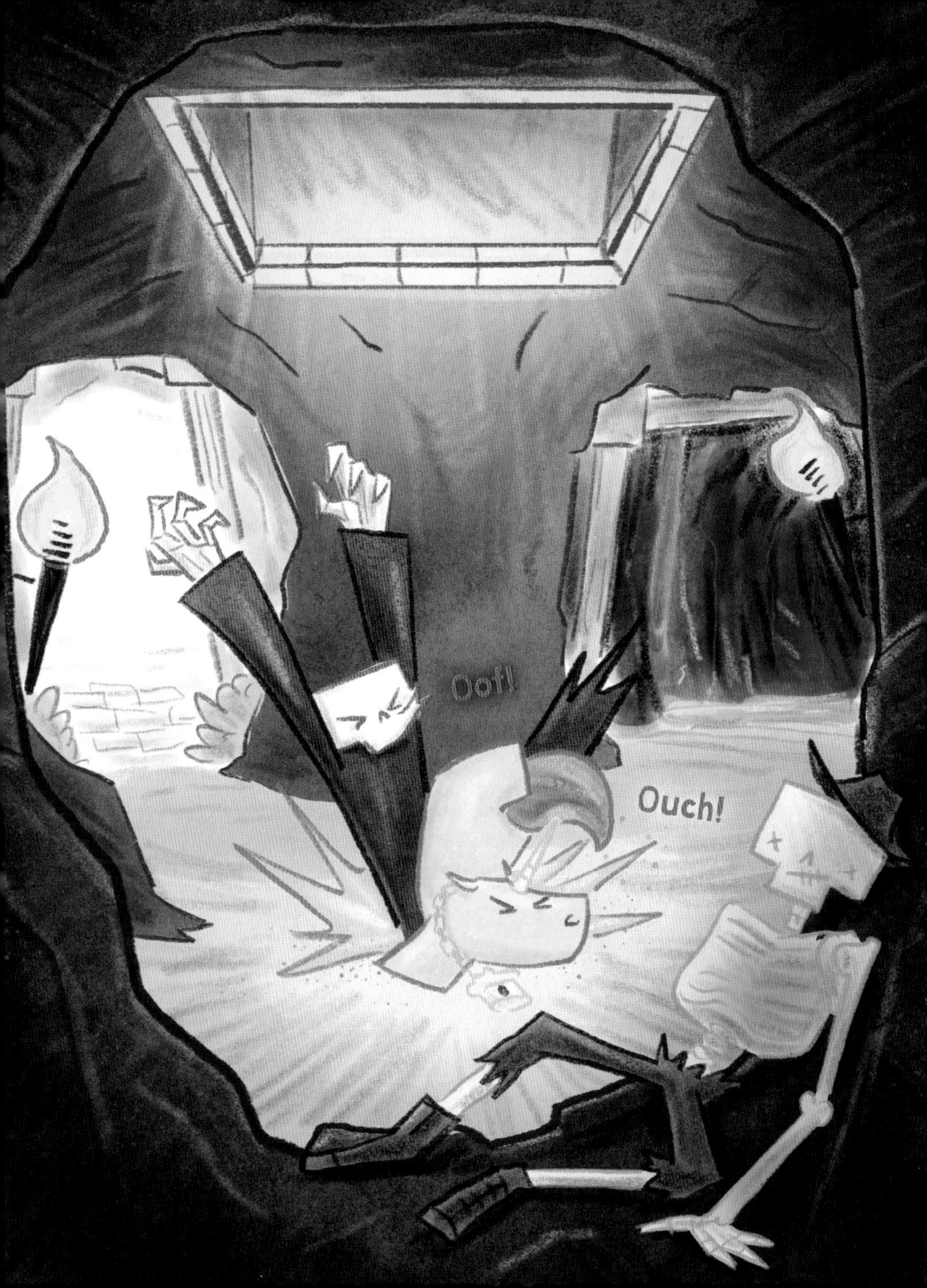
Oof!
Ouch!

Where are we now?
I told you something's fishy about this place.

How are we going to get home now? I have to work tomorrow! I'm going to be in so much trouble.

At least we're doing better than this guy.

Boop.

Boop.

Boop.

Beep!

Nope. This is the way.

FREE HUGS!

No way. Nuh-uh.
But my horn says so!
And where has your horn gotten us so far?
But look—FREE HUGS!
Fact: Unicorns love hugs! This has to be the way!
FREE HUGS!
That's obviously a trap!

I just think you hate hugs.

Why do you hate listening to reason?

Look at this way!

It's got nice walking paths with nice statues and nice benches and nice flowers . . .

That way is smelly and scary and probably full of sewage!

Why do I get the feeling you don't want to solve my super-mega important unicorn family quest AT ALL?!

I'm just asking my pal to help me on a super-cool quest about my ancestors—trying to learn something about my heritage.

I thought it'd be fun, and I thought you'd care.
Ergh!

Maybe I'm a little tired of constantly being wrapped up in your drama! Maybe you could help *me* out sometimes? You come and take over MY house! You don't do anything. You don't clean up. You don't cook. You don't help. You don't know how to do anything for yourself!

Classic unicorn:
selfish, vain, spoiled, careless,
USELESS DRAMA KING!
And you wanna
know the truth?

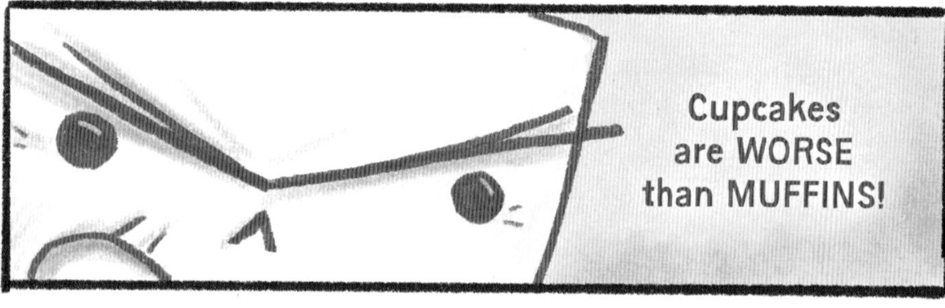
Cupcakes
are WORSE
than MUFFINS!

GASP!
Muffins?

Take that back!

Nuh-uh.

Take that back!

No.

THAT'S IT!

What the—?
RRRRRAAAAAH!

thunk!

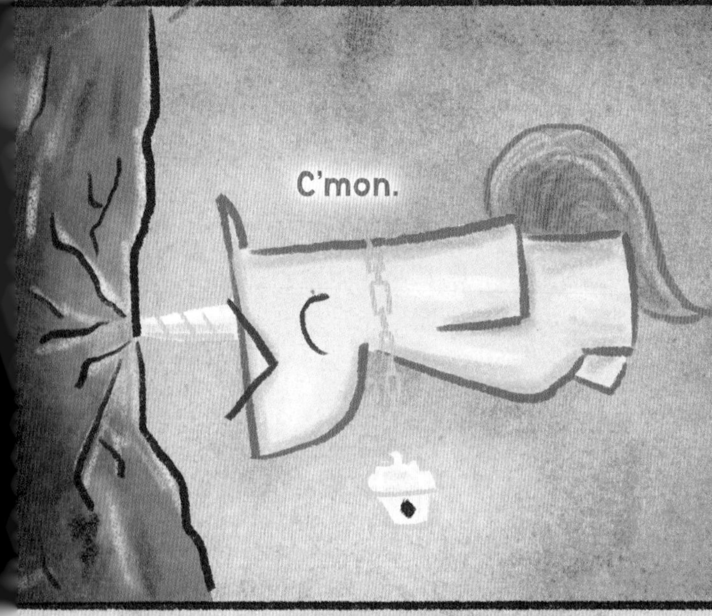
C'mon.

Bravo. Is this
how your unicorn
ancestors acted?

Get me out of here!

Not until you say you're sorry for being a selfish jerk.

I should be sorry? I'm the one who gives my friendship unconditionally. No chores required! I thought we were best friends! Little did I know, you were tallying up all the things you hated about me!

Good luck getting to the club by yourself.

ERGH!

THE ONLY THING I'M SORRY FOR IS BEING FRIENDS WITH YOU!

You don't mean that.

You want
help???

HERE
YOU GO!
AH!

CRASH!

Get this dead
guy off me!

Uh-oh! Watch out for those torches.

BANG!

singe

AH! My tail is on fire!

Stop running! You're going to burn this place down.
FREE

Hold still. I'll smother it with this really dry wooden sign!
FREE HUGS!

crack!
Oh, jeez. I think I'm making it worse.
Oh, man.
whoosh!
whoosh!
AH!
AH!

I'm still on fire!
Everything's on fire!
I don't think this tunnel is structurally sound.
crack!
Ouch!
SMACK!
HEY!
sploosh!

GASP!
sploosh!
sploosh!
sploosh!

The tunnel is caving in!
whoosh!
whoosh!

RUMBLE!

Death?

CHAPTER 9

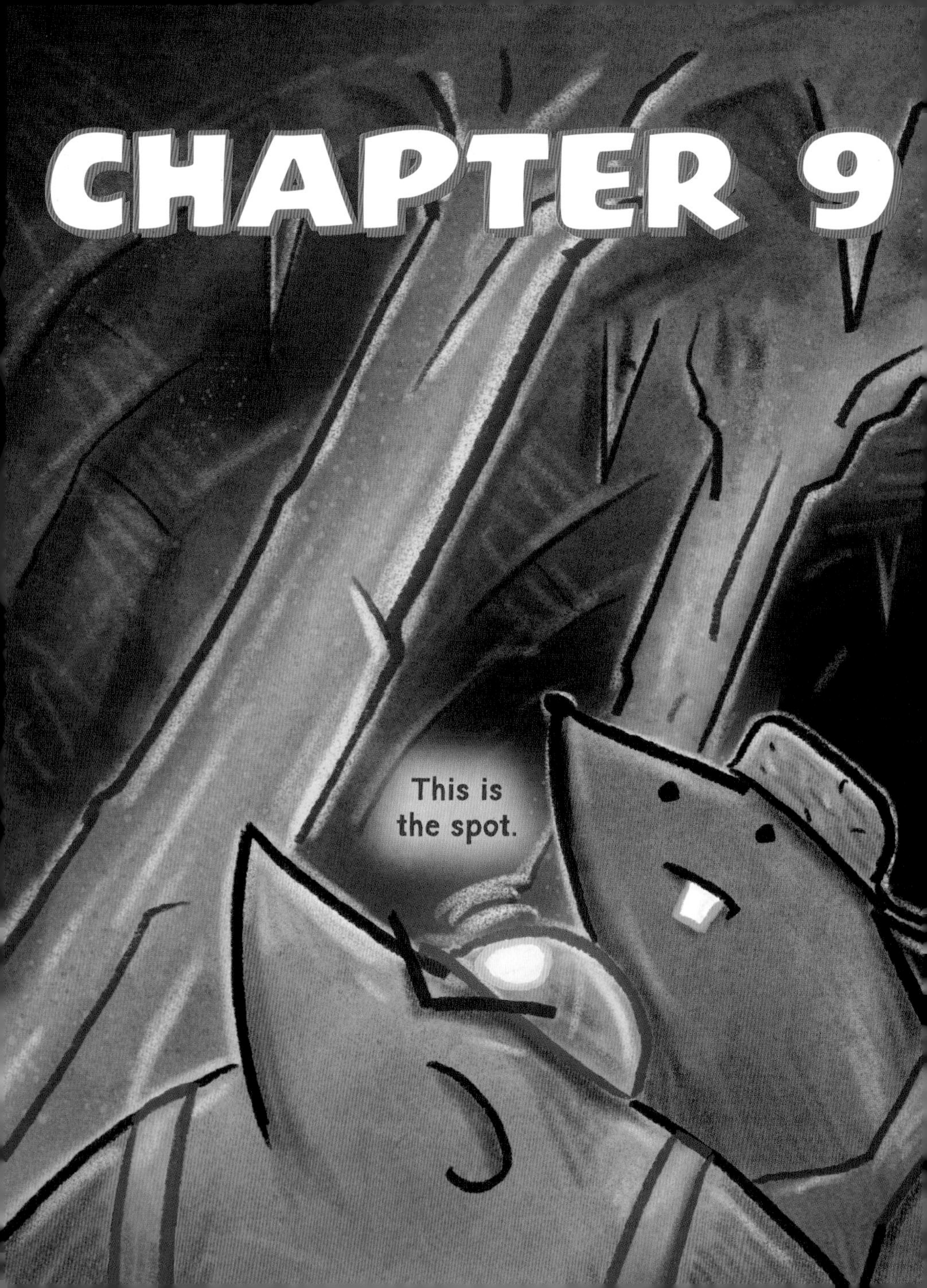

This is the spot.

If we can't go to their party, we'll bring the party to us!

So we'll just . . . start?

I've actually prepared a few words for this occasion.

Sheesh. Get it over with.
Yes!

Here we stand. Four outcasts. Four criminals. Banished
for our sins and selfish actions. Banished for trying to
be friends. Banished just for wanting to be noticed;
wanting to be appreciated; wanting to be loved. Our
journey to this point has been a long one. We've had a
long time to reflect on our actions and how they may
have hurt those we were trying to befriend. Those
whose attention we so desperately sought. We come
from humble beginnings, simple nature-loving
gardeners and groundskeepers. Our time above was
spent soaked in sunshine and happiness. Our time
underground has been far from pleasant. It is cold and
dark and full of spiders. Sometimes it really smells
down here . . . like really While we have stuck
together as a group changed in our own
respect. We have and more resilient,
but at the same time ve lost our smile
and positive outlc hment has been
difficult, but we with us a way
back to the surf on and start
fresh. Fresher kes we only

And then . . .

Ummm . . .

I can't read
my writing.

YADDA-YADDA!
BOO-HOO!
Let's get this show
on the road!

Can we see the plan one more time?
It's simple. We're bringing the garden to the underground.
Above ground
Weak Spots!
Underground
SMASH
BOOM!
YAY!

We bash these pillars, and the garden should fall straight down to us. Then it's ours!
We'll finally be crashing *their* stupid party! Get it? AH-HAHA!

HIT IT!

CH'NK!

CLANK!

TH'NK!

CRACK!

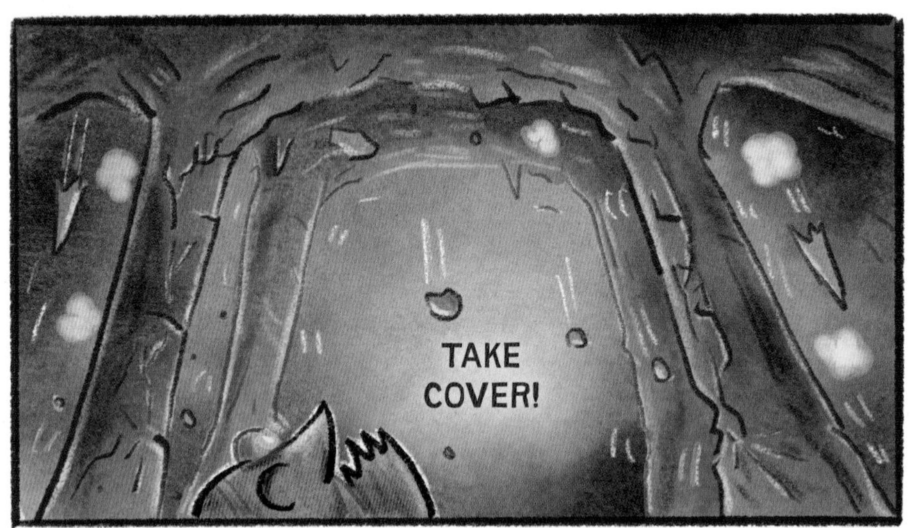
TAKE
COVER!

Hey, it's raining
rocks.

THUNK!

AH!

RUMBLE!
RUMBLE!
RUMBLE!
It's happening! Our plan is working!
You see the light, too? It's coming down!
Ah h'ar!

rumble rumble

rumble rumble

BRRRRRUUUNCH!

BOOM!

WHERE ARE THEY???
They should be here. Today is the day.
Same as every year.

Is this some
sort of prank?

They're gone!
The Golden Cupcake
is gone! No!

We're never
getting out of here.

sniff

sniff

BAAAAH!

What do we
do now?

sob sob

sniiiiiiiiiiiiff

We wait.

We
plan.

We prepare.

And I know deep down in my gut that at some point at least one dumb unicorn is going to come trotting down here with the Golden Cupcake to go to their party.
AND when they do, we'll be ready!

CHAPTER 10

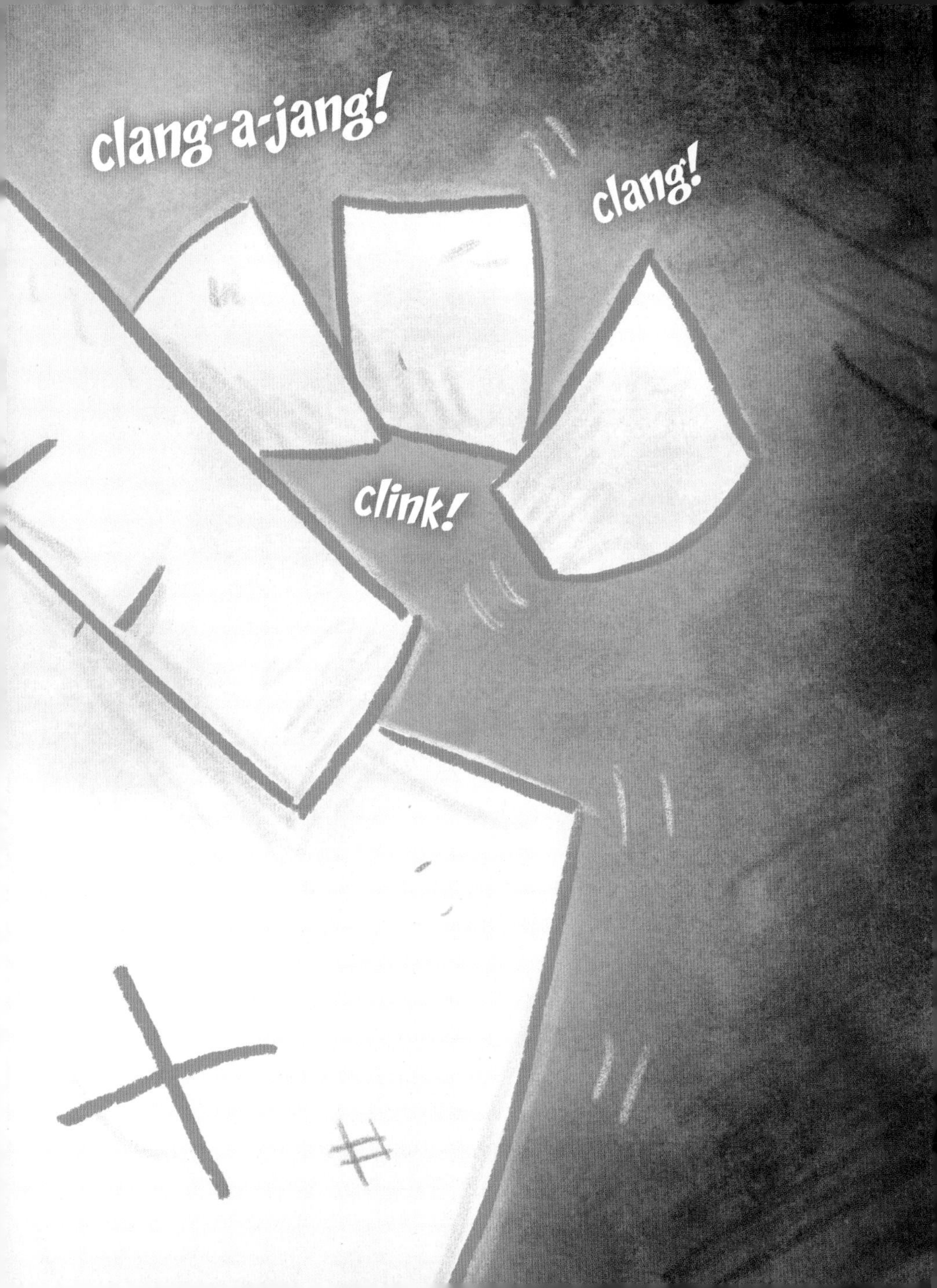

clang-a-jang!

clang!

clink!

cling-a-ting!

Grrrrr . . .

tang!

Okay, horn. I'm really trusting you. If it was ANYTHING ELSE, I would've turned back by now!
Blech! What am I stepping on?

Just try to ignore it.

I'm almost there.

It'll all be worth it.

It's only getting a little deeper.

Bleh!
I got some in my mouth.

BLARB!!!

sploosh!

Huh?

Guh?

BLURB!

AH!
splash!

Thank goodness this chain's here.

Oh, no . . .
This probably isn't going anywhere good . . .
FLUSH!

Oof!
k'dnk!

All right. Where am I now?

I really hope this leads to the club.

Okay. This isn't so bad.
Kinda relaxing, actually.
squeak
squeak
squeak

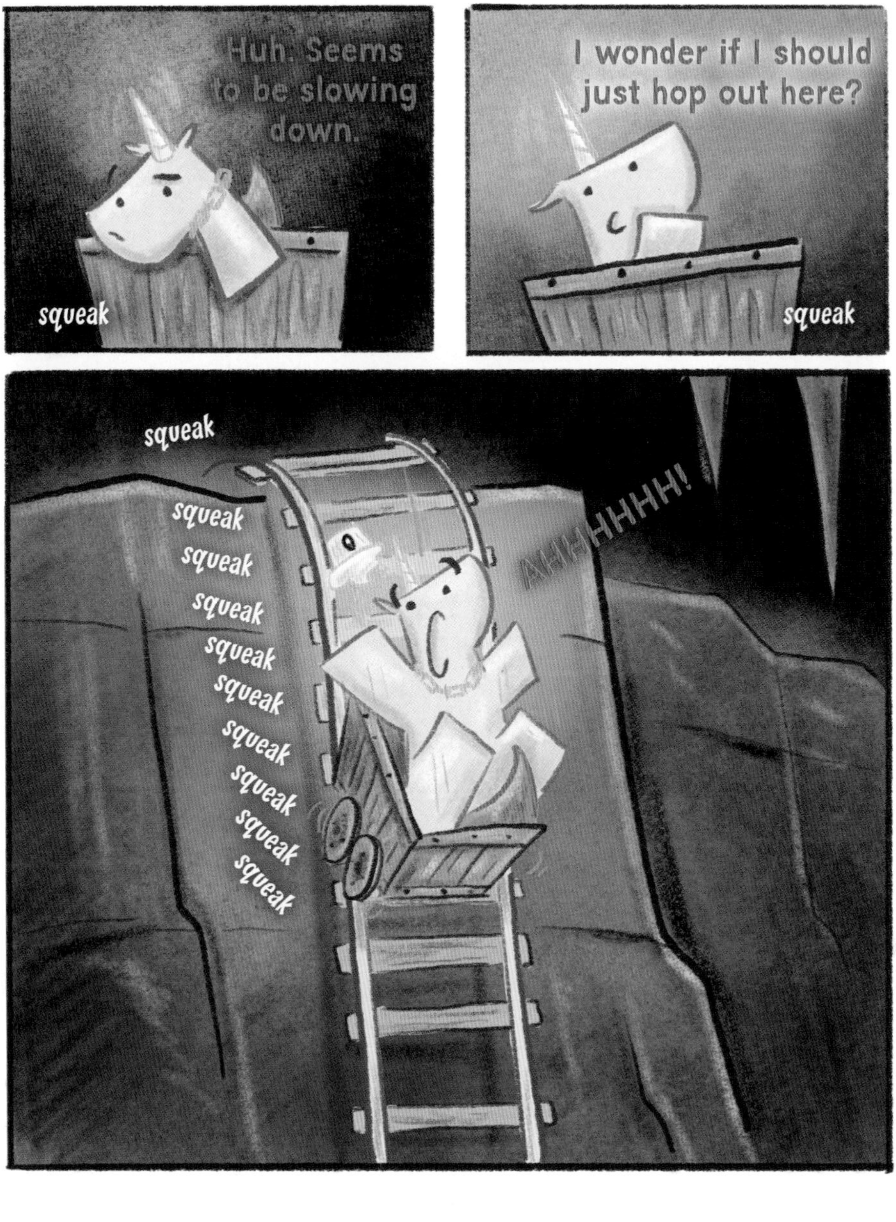

squeak

squeak
squeak
squeak
squeak
squeak
squeak
squeak
squeak
squeak

AHHHHHHHH!

WHAT IS
THAT?

KUNK!
squeak
squeak

squeak
AHHHH!
KUNK!
squeak
KUNK!

Is it safe yet?
squeak
squeak

What's the purpose of those thin—
squeak
squeak

G'oh!

MUFFINS 4EVA!
DOWN WITH HORNS
UNICORNS DROOL
CORN SMEL
Is this where my ancestors lived? Not how I pictured it. I thought there'd be more bling, and definitely less graffiti.
Hmmm . . . My horn isn't as glowy.
Did I make a wrong turn somewhere?
squeak
clunk

RAWR!
FAH!
RAWR!
What's that???
A yeti?
G'oh!
SMOKE
squeak
squeak

AH! Mousetraps!
AH! Snakes!
AH! Cacti!
AH! Clowns!
AH! Flamethrowers!
MORE FREE HUGS

pant
pant
pant
huff
huff
huff
I just want
to dance.
SPROING!

WAAAAAH!

Is that Death?

DEATH!!!

Who's he with?
Can't he hear me?

Nice!
I'm going
to land right
in the club!
SMASH!

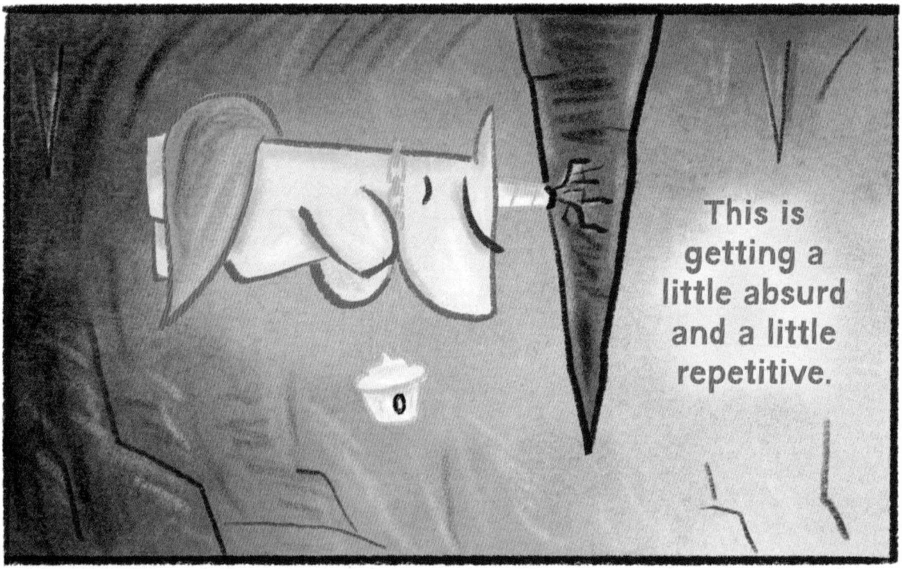

This is getting a little absurd and a little repetitive.

crack
Why is my horn taking me here? When will I know what to do?
crack

AHHHHHH!

Oof!

Uuuuuunnhh . . .
Where am I now?

Some sort of garbage pit?

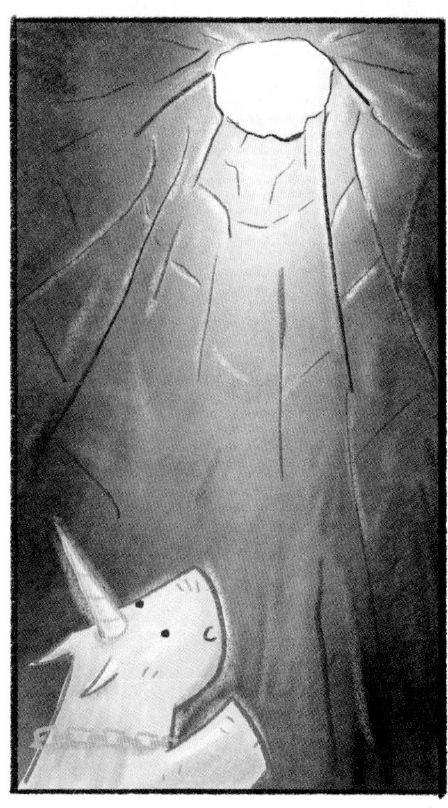

Hellooooo?
HELLO?!

HEY! Sparkles here!
Used to be famous,
but now not so much!
(But you never know
when my comeback will be!)
cricket
cricket
Anybody?

What have I gotten
myself into?

Maybe my parents
were wrong about me.

Maybe I'm not
a good-enough
unicorn.

Maybe I
don't know
exactly what
to do.

CHAPTER 11

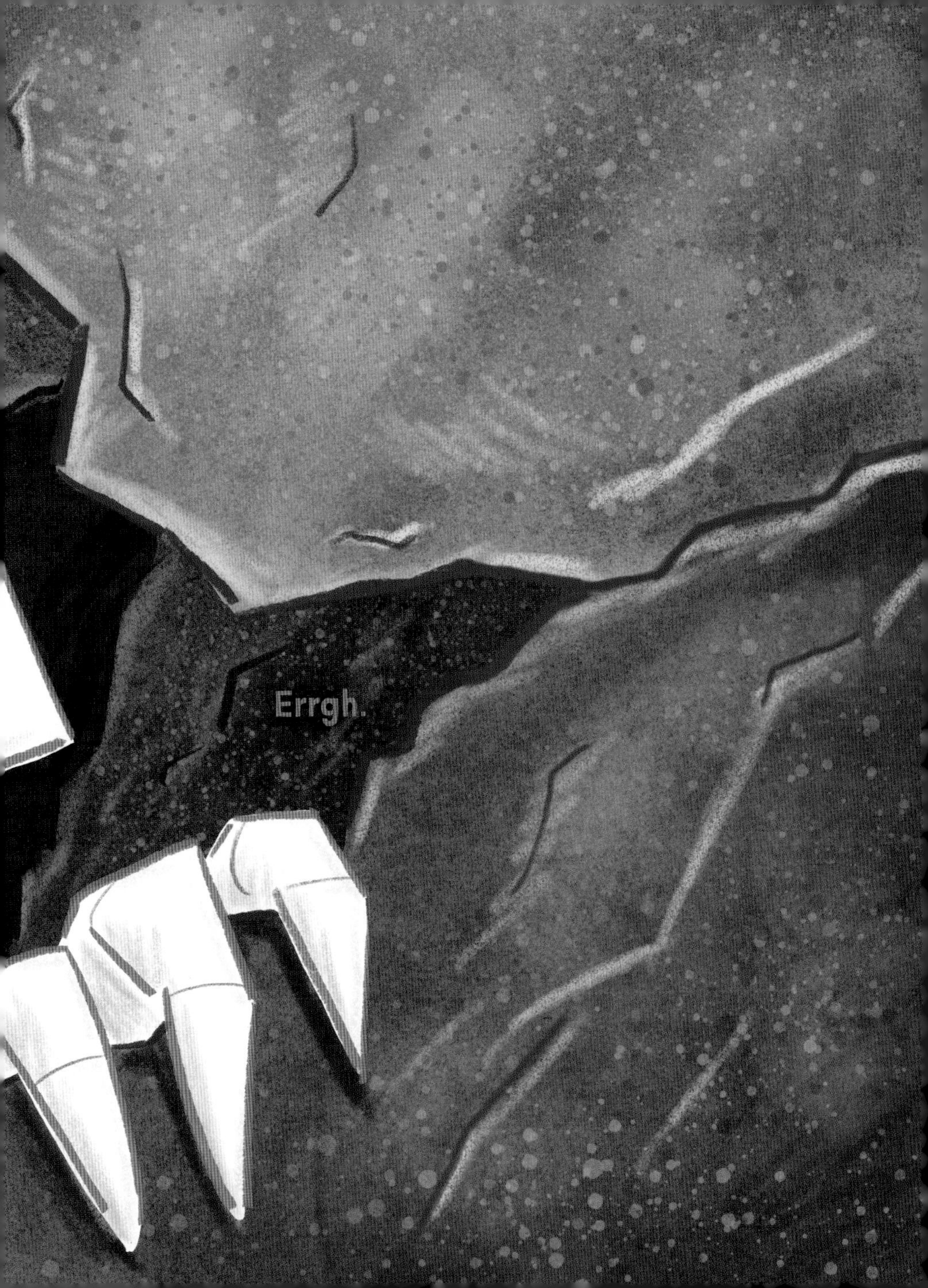
Errgh.

Hurgh!

HARRR!

Hoooo!
POP!

Stupid
Sparkles . . .

. . . and his stupid
glowing horn.

We could be at home
right now playing vids!

Now I'm stuck
down here.

Thanks for dragging me out dancing.
Look at all the dancing we're doing!
Thanks for dressing me up like a fool
for people to laugh at me!
Thanks for pushing
me into this weird
underground maze!
Have we learned anything
about your stupid
family and ancestors?

Some "friend"
you are.

Maybe I'll
find some
new friends.

Who am I kidding? I'll just
go back to being alone.
sniff

Alone.
Alone.

Alone.
Alone.
Alone.

Alone.
Loner.
Alone.
All alone.
He-he.

Who said that?

Ouch!
bing!

Sparkles?
skitter

snicker
He-he!
Har!

I don't know who's
out there, but you
should be . . .

. . . uh . . . um . . .

. . . SUPER scared
of me!

Oh, yeah? Says who?
Uhhhhh . . .

Says Death!
(And my
super-scary
touch of
death! And
even scarier
paperwork!)

HAHA!
HAR! HAR!
He-he!
Yuk-yuk!
Well, guess what?
What?
We're not afraid of death.

GAH!
HAHA!

CHAPTER 12

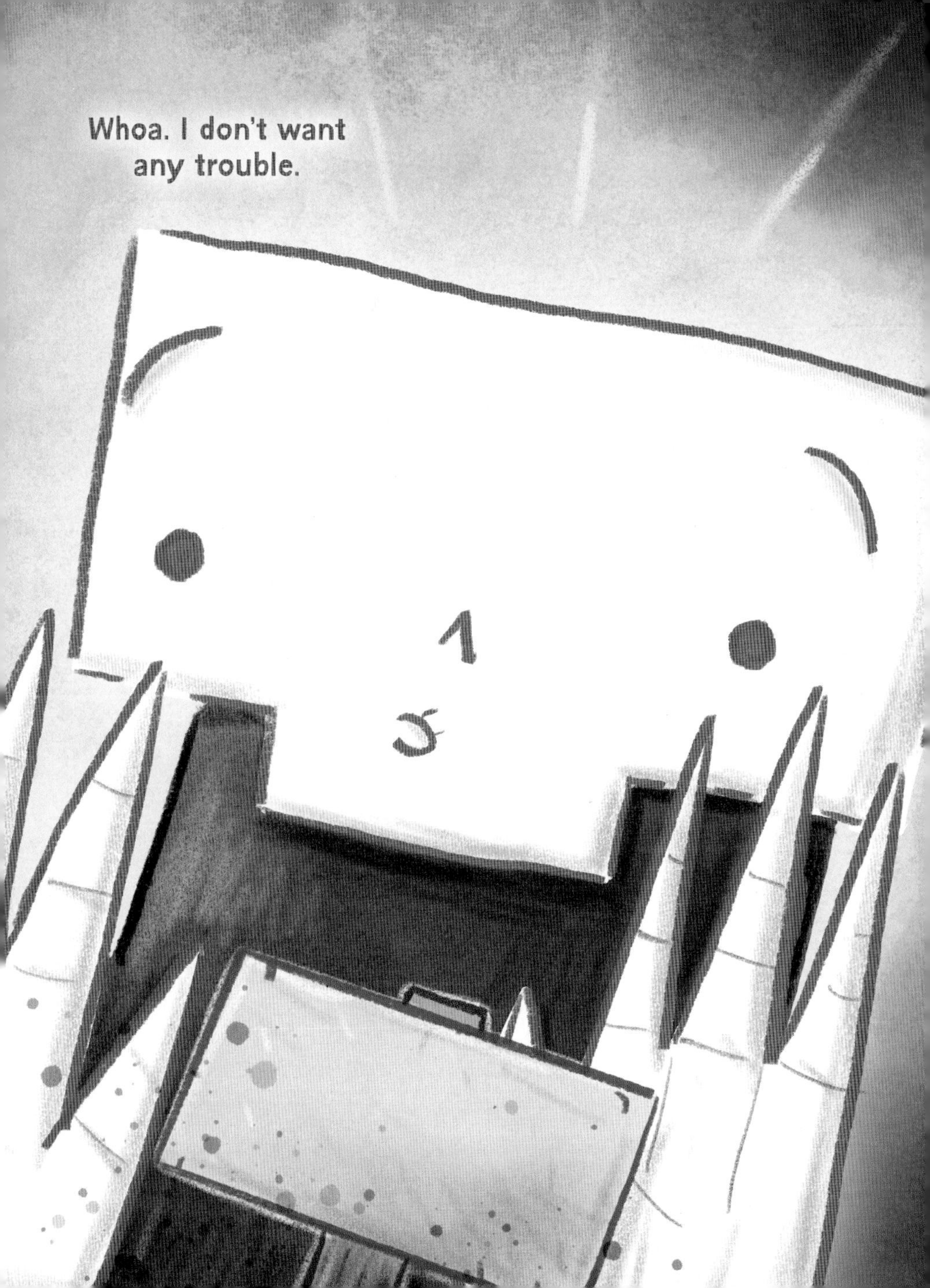
Whoa. I don't want
any trouble.

I'm just looking for
my friend Sparkles.
Pudgy unicorn wearing
some sort of ancient Golden
Cupcake that his unicorn
parents gave to him. I think he
thinks that it has some sort of
magical powers or something.

I mean, that's if we're even friends anymore.

We kinda had a fight looking for some special underground place to dance or something.

If he dances there, he becomes an adult unicorn or some sort of uni-stallion. I don't know, exactly.

But I guess this was a long time coming. Who'd want to be friends with Death anyway?

A unicorn with a fancy
Golden Cupcake being friends
with someone like me?!

I know, I know.
It all sounds
so wacky!

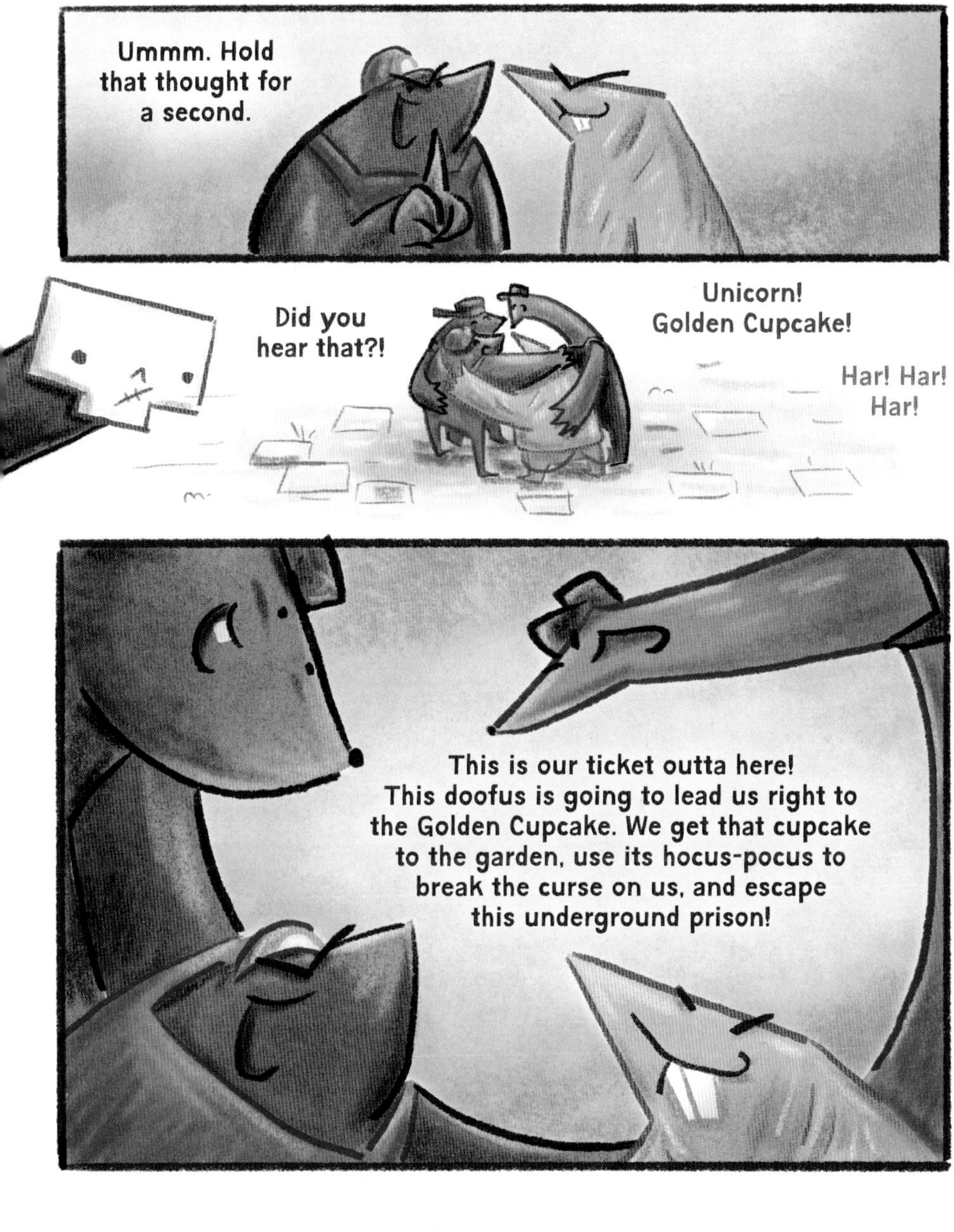

This is our ticket outta here!
This doofus is going to lead us right to
the Golden Cupcake. We get that cupcake
to the garden, use its hocus-pocus to
break the curse on us, and escape
this underground prison!

Okay. Pranks on three.
One.
Two.
H'erm.

PRANKS!

So first off, niiiice cloak. It really brings out your . . . uh . . . eye sockets. Yeah!
Why, thank you. No one's ever told me that before.

Why don't you hang with us? We'll help you find your stupi . . . endous unicorn friend. Heh.

That's so kind! What do you four do for fun down here?

PRANKS!
Oh. Wow.
We built this entire maze to prank our old friends.
Huh. That seems like it'd take a while.

Yeah! We're going to get back at those self-centered, oppressive, one-horned—
SHHH!

Haha! Pranks! Just ignore Brown. He doesn't know what he's talking about. Heh.

So, pranks? Like, not replacing the TP roll when it's done?

slap!
First off, you can't call it TP. You gotta call it something cooler.

What do you guys call it?

BUM
BARK!

Oh. I don't know . . .

What if work finds out about this?

Look, friend—I can tell you're a decent ghoul. You seem like a guy who cares about his friend, even if you're responsible for taking everyone's life and loved ones away from them. So why not take one night off from being a rule-follower and mix it up with us! We don't hurt anybody—it's just pranks!

Yeah, I guess that'd be all right. It's just pranks!

sploosh!
splat!

Ptoie!
Ptoie!

Heh!
He-he-he.
Wow! Good aim! That's a real thick loogie, too!

shake
shake

fffffshhh!

DEATH RULEZ
Great job! Good composition!

HAR! HAR!
HAR! HAR!

NO
LOITERING
It's funny because we put this sign here.
Heh-heh.

HAR!
HAR!
HAR!
beep
beep
beep

What's with the beeping?

Something set off our traps.

Probably Sparkles being his usual dramatic self.
Oh, that dramatic Sparkles and your Golden Cupcake.

Say, I've got an idea.

Why don't we play an
equally dramatic prank
on your friend Sparkles?

PRRRANKS!
KEEP OFF
GRASS!

CHAPTER 13

Sparkles?
Huh?
D?

Is that you down there?

Ho, boy—
am I glad to
see you!

Um . . . yeah . . . me, too.

Hurry up, will you!
Arrgh!
Don't
rush me!

Who are you
talking to?

Oh, it's
nobody.
Get on
with it!

You
sure?

Oh. It's just some new friends I made.
snicker
Har! Har!

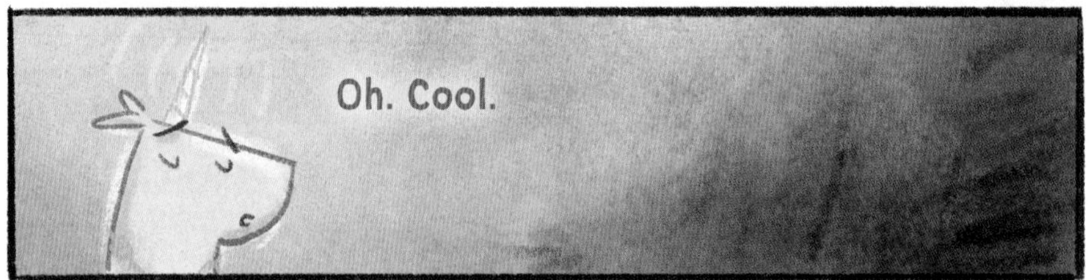
Oh. Cool.

Here. Put this on and I'll pull you up.

Um, are these clean?

Oh, yeah. Totally super clean.
BWA-HA-HA!

SHHH!

Blech!

Hurk!

You almost in?
Almo—

Err!
Arrgh!
Man, am I so glad to see you. I was worried you were still mad at me.
Oh. These are your friends?

Yup.
My REAL
friends.

Unlike you
jerk unicorns!

Well, I'm the
only unicorn
I've ever
known.

And I'd like to think I'm
a pretty cool dude.

Right, D?

Is trying to stab
your best friend
with your horn
considered cool?

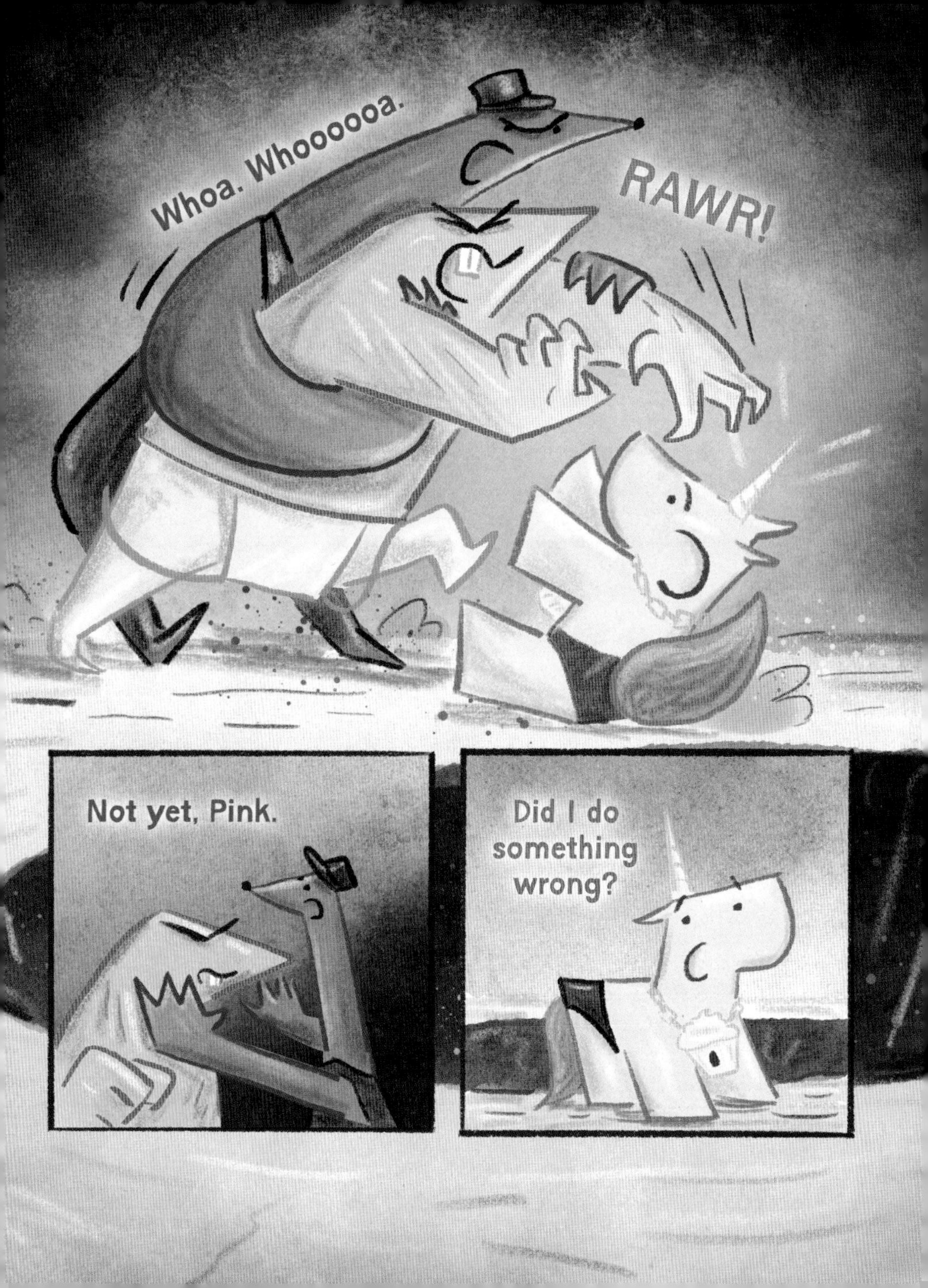

Whoa. Whoooooa.

RAWR!

Something wrong?

Heh. This 'corn a comedian or something?

I'll have you know my stand-up special was both a critical and commercial success.

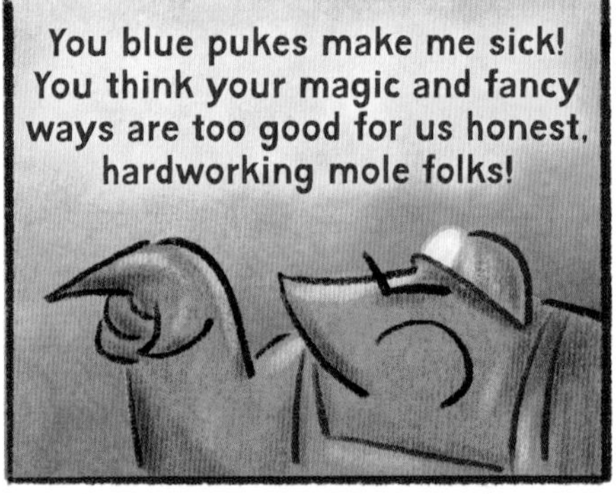
You blue pukes make me sick! You think your magic and fancy ways are too good for us honest, hardworking mole folks!

You use people again and again!
Shhh.

whisper whisper

Har! Har! Har!
You're right.

Am I missing
something???

Sorry. Just a little
conversation
between friends.

And, yes, you
are missing
something . . .

Or rather, you
will be!

I'm sorry I lost my cool earlier.
I just really want to figure out
what all this horn stuff means.

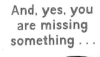

Heh-heh.

Now hand over the cupcake!

Hey!
swipe!

What are you doing???
If you can't figure out what to do with it, maybe you don't deserve it!

CREEEEEEEAAK!

STOP!
I'm sorry!

Hey, look! Is that a hip
dance party
over there?
Where?

AHA!
No!
ching!

There you
go, pals.

Finally.

We can see
the sun.
After so much time
and so much heartbreak.

Finally.

Finally.

FINALLY, WE CAN BREAK THIS STUPID CURSE! WE CAN GET OUT OF HERE!

Please. It's my only connection to my heritage. I've got a feeling that it's for something really special.

Heeeeeere you go.

sniff Thanks.

You know how much this means to m—

PRANKS! Just kidding!

Haha!

Quit it!

Har! Har!

HAHAHA!

HAHA!

Heh!

This isn't funny! Please, can I have it back?

Oh. We're sorry.

Right, gang?
So sorry.

Sorry that your ancestors were all jerks!

GASP!

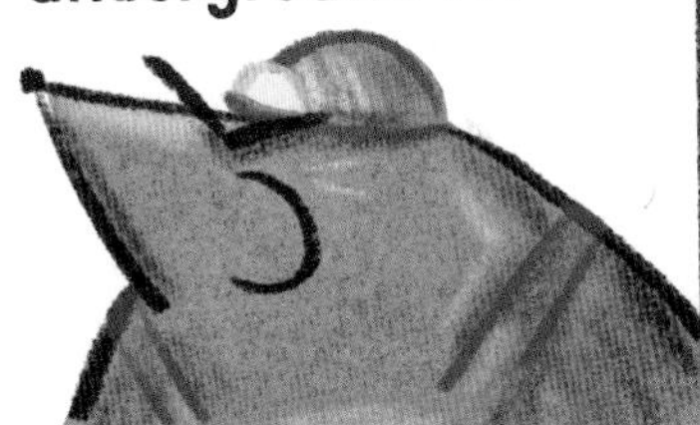
And just like they
pushed and trapped us
underground . . .

. . . I think
it's time we
return the
favor!

I just wanted to
know my past . . .
and boogie
down.

Maybe we're taking
this prank too far?
Nope.

NO!

Let's get to the
garden, crack this
cupcake open, and
bust out of here!

CHAPTER 14

This is not how I thought my quest would go. Is this what my parents knew would happen?

sigh
So tired.

Maybe I'll just lie here for a bit.

Rest . . .
my . . .
eyes . . .
ZZZZZ . . .

Whoa . . .
I made it!
Woo-hoo!

Why are we stopping?
You're not supposed to be here. Have you really earned this? Quitters aren't welcome.
We eat quitters for breakfast.
Wait. What?

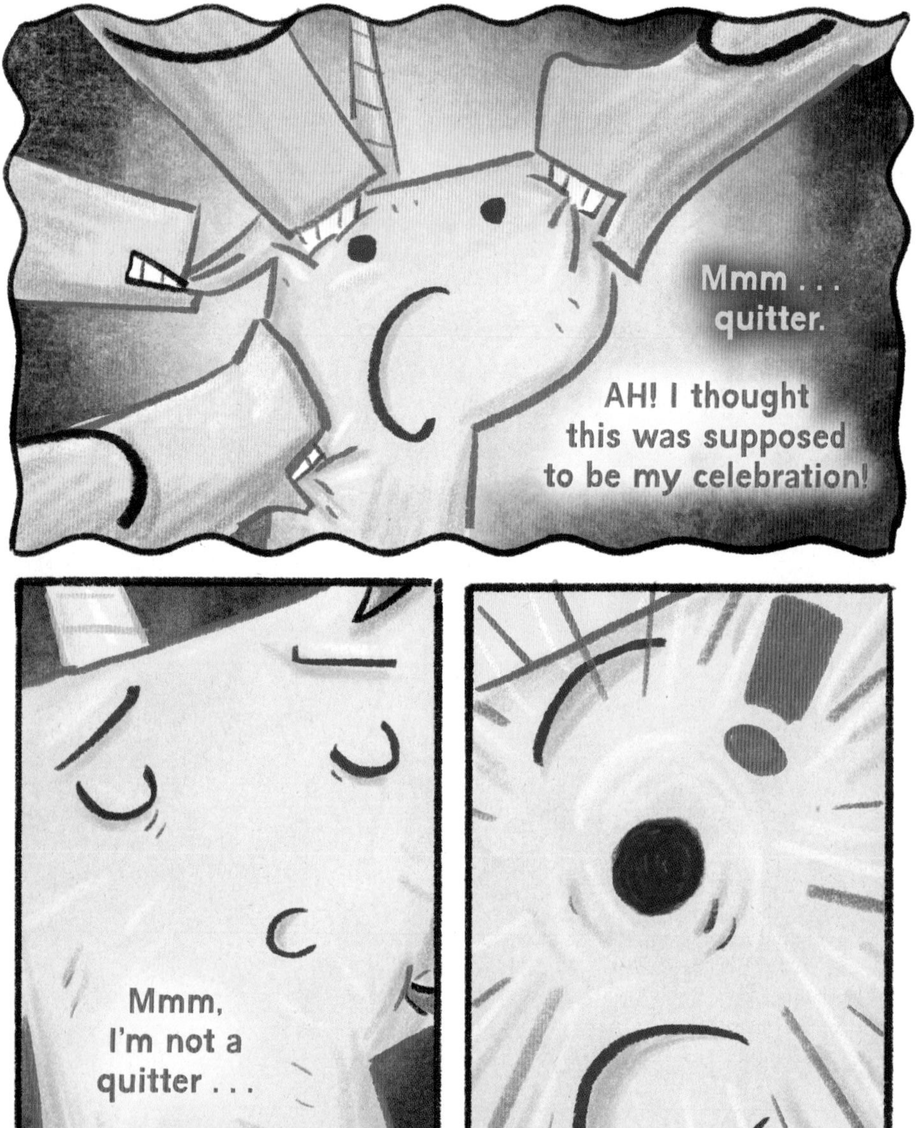

Mmm . . . quitter.

AH! I thought this was supposed to be my celebration!

WHA

Get
off me!

I may be sweet, but
I'm no chew toy!
Get back here, you
vermin!
RAAAHH!

Another
pipe?

Huh.

My horn's telling me maybe those rats were on to something.

bloop!
bloop!
bloop!

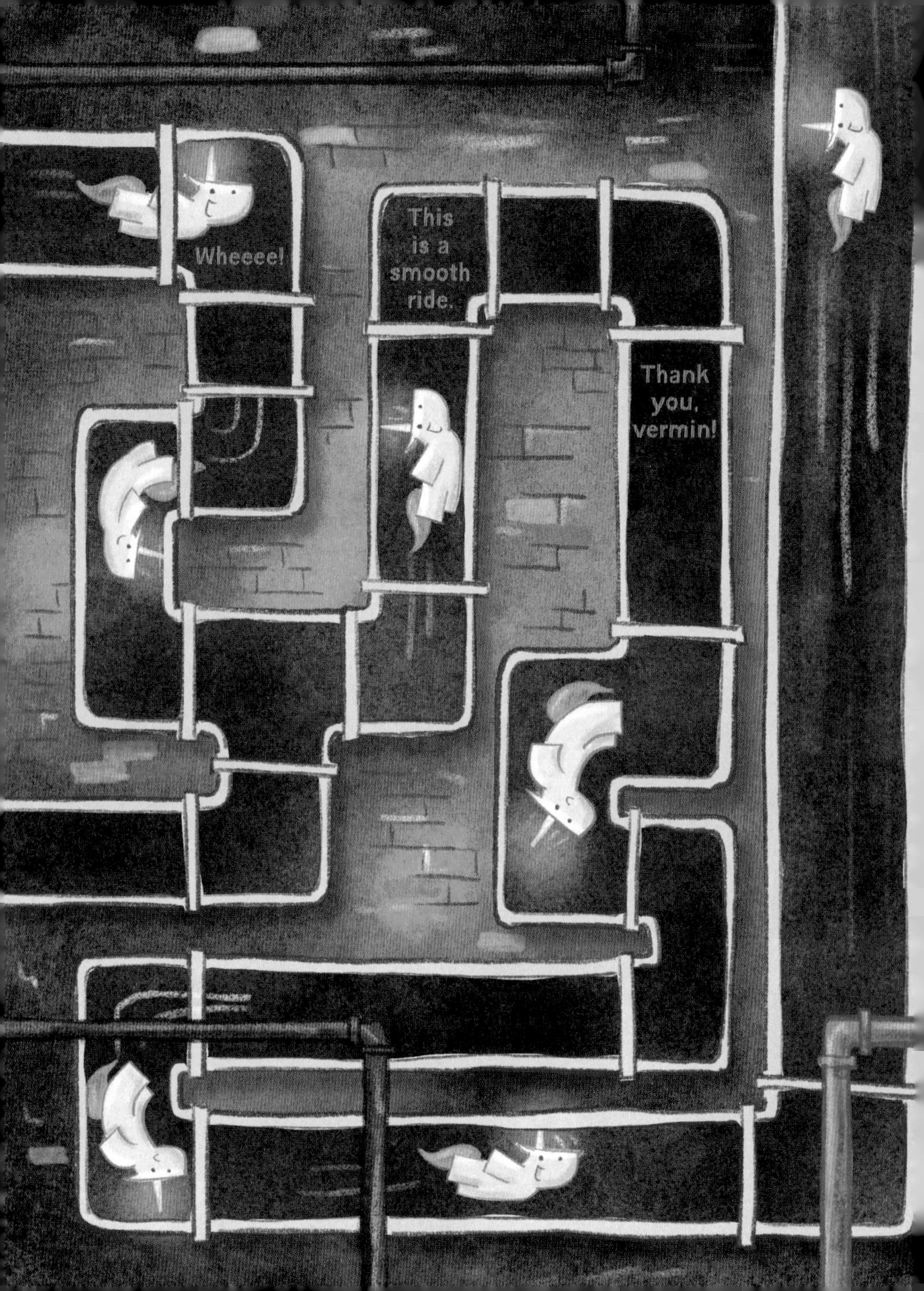
Wheeee!
This is a smooth ride.
Thank you, vermin!

YES!

Just goes to
show—never
discount the
little guys.

No way.
I'm almost there!
Woo-hoo!
It's like that
pipe is some
sort of warp zone.

Time to get my bling back! Then it's time to DANCE!

Oops!

thk!
thk!
thk!
Hurk!

Oooouch.

RUMBLE
RUMBLE
RUMBLE

CRUNCH

C'mon!
Really?
thk!

CHAPTER 15

ERRR!

Why won't this thing open?!

We're in the garden.

By the great dragon.

Herm.

ARRRGH! No, Pink!
There's no button.

Maybe it's just for unicorns?

WHAT?!

You prankin' us?

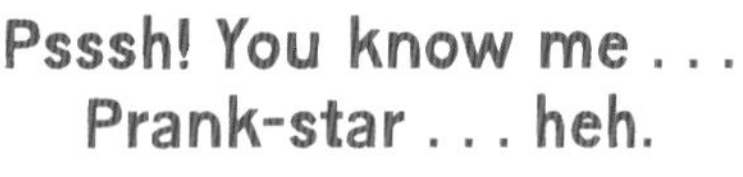

Psssh! You know me . . . Prank-star . . . heh.

Ha! For a moment there, I thought you were in cahoots with that unicorn.

Well, we are roomies . . . and maybe we did cross a line. Sure, from what you've told me, those old unicorns seem like mega jerks, but Sparkles just wanted to dance . . . and something to do with his parents. I knew I should've listened better.

Alls we know is that the 'corns we knew were pompous poops who cursed us underground. We're just looking for revenge!

And our freedom. Let's not forget that part.

Remember the sun?

The sun was so nice.

I don't know. Maybe we should get him out of that pit? Maybe he can help you guys? No pranks. For realsies.

GAH! FINE
BUT! He'll have to earn our trust. The moment he's trouble, he's gone. Capisce?
YESSIR!

Phew. Oh man. That is a BIG load off my chest. I mean, I've definitely been having so much fun doing these hilarious pranks, but I have not been feeling good at all about pushing Sparkles back down th me and him have our disagreements, and he can drive me cra a little on the messy side, but he is my pal and we've had together. I guess I was a little too excited taking the night taking the night off from being good. I never realized h od prank could be. At the same time I guess we just took ittle too far. I'm a rule follower, so doing th thi ally exciting. Maybe I got carried away a t I'm down here, and that was to help Sparkles, and act opposite. Sheesh! look at me ramble on and

Okay. Okay. Save that lovefest for later. Let's go get yer 'corn friend before the rats get 'im.
I liked your rant.
H'ruh?

rumble!

Huh?

RUMBLE!

BO

OM!

DEATH!?!
He got out!!!
HE GOT OUT???
HELP! Even though I'm still—
rumble rumble rumble

Mmrf!

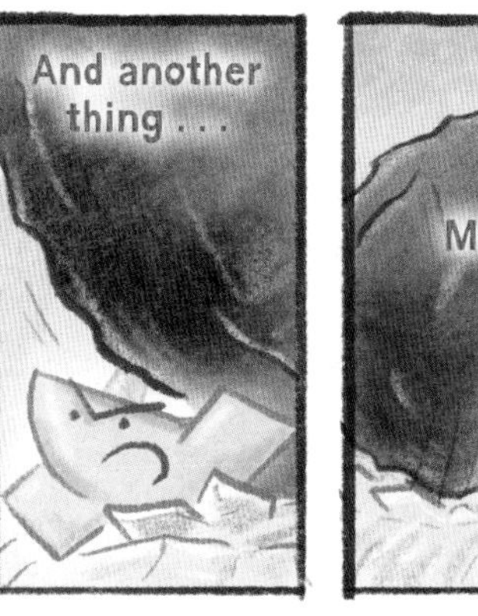
And another thing . . .

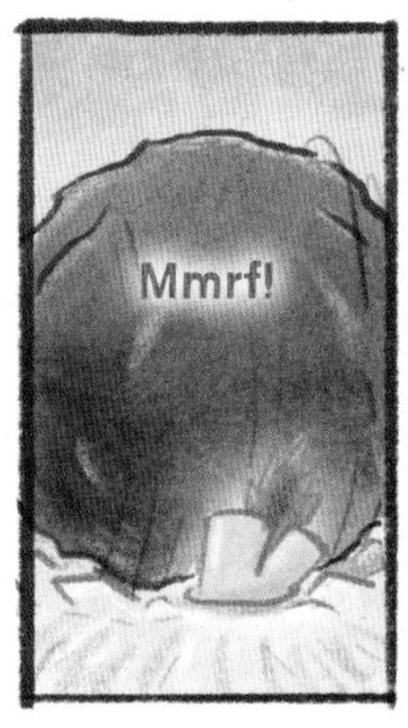
Mmrf!

. . . I'm going to get my bling back!

ARH!
CRUNCH!

RAWR!

GAH!
Oof!

poke!
thunk!
crunch!
RUMBLE!

You don't even know what it's for!

It's for me! Not a bunch of jerk thieves.

I know you tricked Death into not being my friend anymore!

You did that to yourself. Typical unicorn. Never your doin's.

What do you mean, "typical"? I'm the only one there is.

I just want to make my parents proud!!!

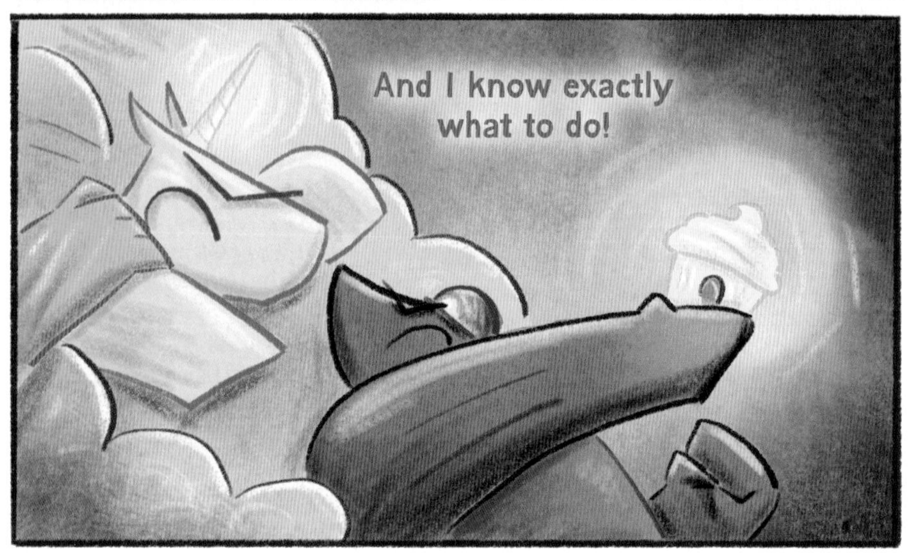
And I know exactly what to do!

HIYA!

HURK!

SQUISH!

bewwwww!

MY BLING!

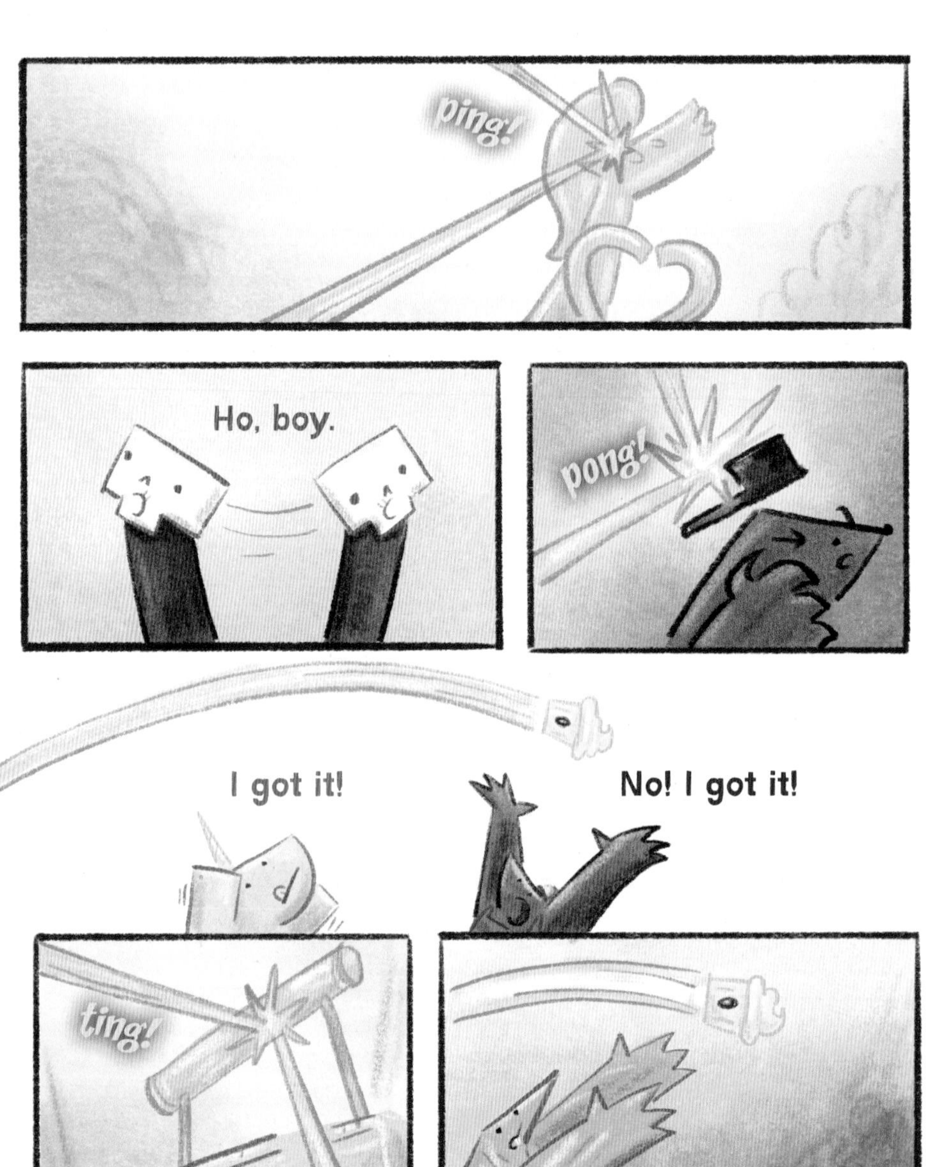
ping!
Ho, boy.
pong!
I got it!
No! I got it!
ting!

dong!

Please don't
break.

That Golden
Cupcake sure
is bouncy.

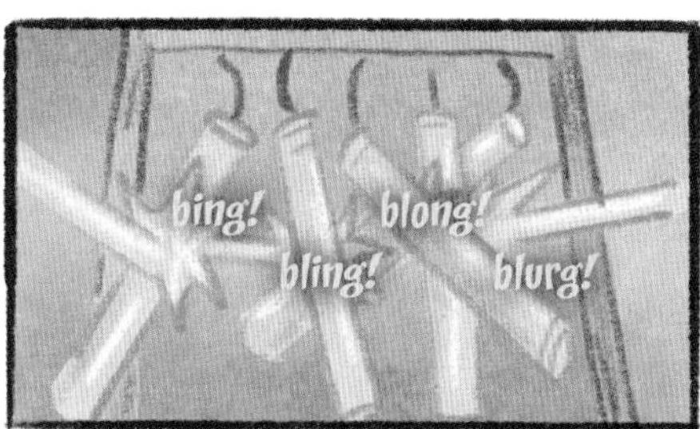
bing!
bling!
blong!
blurg!

bewwwwww!

clank!

Thank cupcakes you caught my bling! Now I can finally become the noble unicorn (or, as I'd like to call it, uni-stallion) I'm meant to be!

Don't think so, 'corny. Death, pal! Hand that over so we can finally break this curse and get out of here.

You'd love that.

He's *our* friend now!

Maybe we can
work this out?

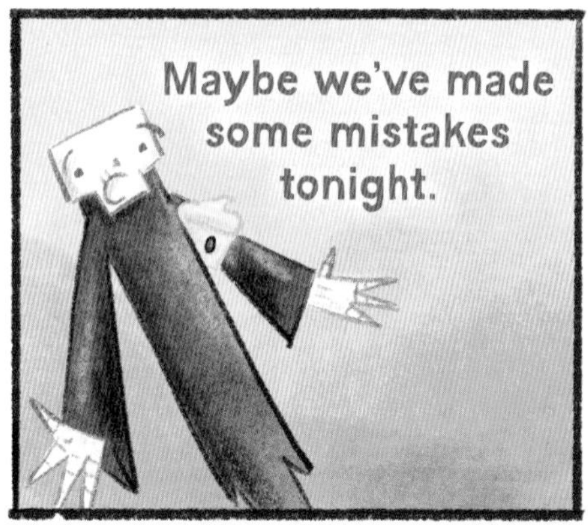
Maybe we've made
some mistakes
tonight.

Maybe we've
done things we
regret.

Maybe we've hurt the
people closest to us.

Maybe we should be
checking in with work. I
mean, they must be wor—

D! Where are you
going with this?
Yeah!

Oh, sorry. I'll get to the point.
Aherm!
Clearly, there's only one way to settle this beef!

A dance-off.

CHAPTER 16

Oh, you're going down.

Think so?

I'll have you know that
I'm the danciest dancer
that's ever danced
the dance floor!
You have no idea, 'corn.

Get ready to get crushed.
My dance world tours
were choreographed by
the BEST in the biz.
crack!

Sheesh. He always
like this?

Yeah, pretty
much. Confidence
can take someone
a long way.

Enough of this
SMACK TALK!
Let's lay down the rules
for this dance-off.

Rules are simple. Pick a song, then dance your little heart out to it. At the end, I pick whoever had the best moves. Winner gets this Sacred Golden Cupcake blingy thingy!

Deal?

Let's see what
you've got.

Ahem!

Hmmm . . .

Urrrrr . . .

Uhhhh, what are
you doing?

I'm
limbering
up!

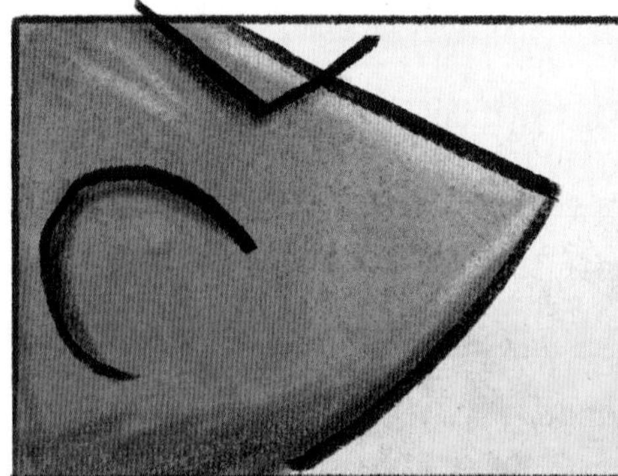
GET ON
WITH IT!

Get ready to
have your butts
blown away!

Here we go!
ROOTIE-TOOTIE BOOTY
RUMP-SHAKER RMX

inhale
Okay, Sparkles. Time to make my forefathers and foremothers proud.

Try to beat this rump-shaker.

Whoo! How's everyone doing tonight?
clap!

shake
shake

Is he disco-dancing?

shuffle

shake
shake
shake

Tee-hee!

It's kinda hypnotic.
You shouldn't be watching this.

Oh, my. That is a LOT of twerking.

Is that even dancing?

I don't think his ancestors would like what he's doing to that statue.

It's going on for so long.
Why can't I watch?

TA-DA!

heave
heave

Okay . . .

Ummm . . .

That was different.

Did you practice?
Yeah, I practiced.

Okay, then.

Uh . . . Good job.
clap
clap
clap

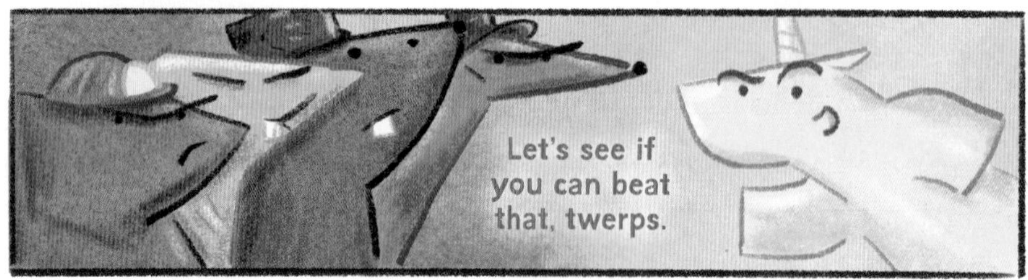
Let's see if you can beat that, twerps.

You have no idea how long we've waited for this.

Ready, boys?

Where did they get those instruments from?

You don't want to know.

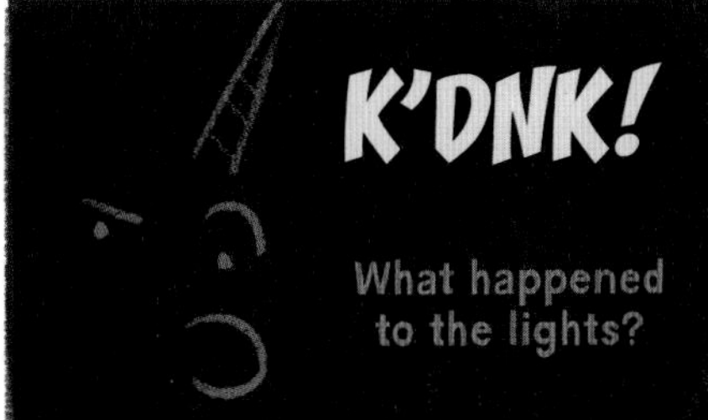
K'DNK!
What happened to the lights?

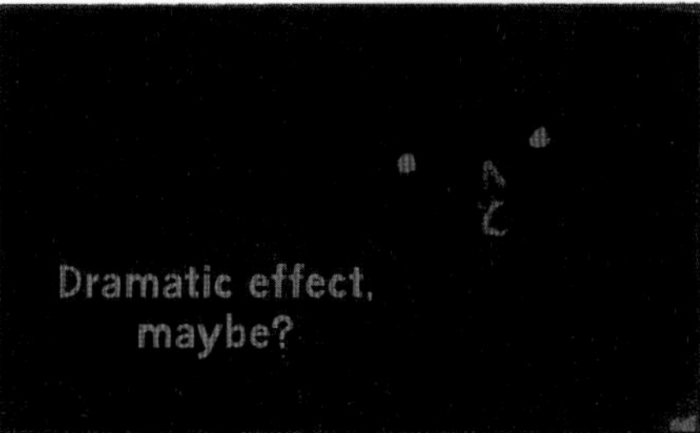
Dramatic effect, maybe?

K'DNK!

This is definitely different from my dance.

This is not what I expected at all.

This is beautiful.

sniff

This is the saddest, most beautiful dance I've ever seen.

Not just the dancing, either. The music is so . . .
Moving.

This is art.
It's like they're telling a story.
ting!

huff
huff

Wow.

I didn't know dancing could make me feel this way.

Yeah, that was pretty good . . .
It'll be a close one.
clap
clap
clap

Yeah . . .

So, who's it going to be, boney?

Your friend who violated half the statues in his ancestors' ancient sacred garden?

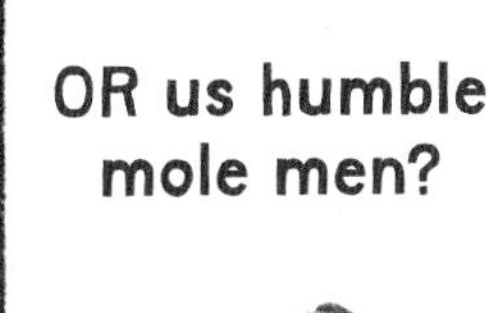
OR us humble mole men?

Pshhh! Please. It's gonna be me.

Who's it gonna be?
Who? Who?
Who's it gonna be?
Who's it gonna be?

ENOUGH ALREADY!

It's gonna be . . .

It's gonna be me.

The
MOLE
MEN!

WHAT?!

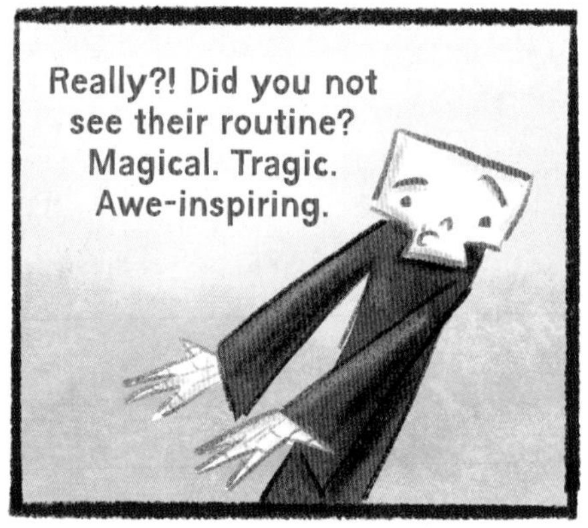
Really?! Did you not see their routine? Magical. Tragic. Awe-inspiring.

I know I saw you crying, too.
I had something in my eye.

Besides, where was all the booty-shaking?

It's not dancing if you're not rump-jumpin'!

Can you put that thing away?

I'm just shaking what my mama gave me.

In your face!

Now where's OUR Golden Cupcake?

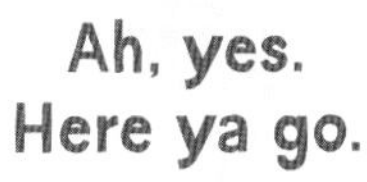

Ah, yes.
Here ya go.

NOOOOO!

No what?

THAT'S MY CUPCAKE!

Dude!
GASP!

My parents gave this to me . . .

We won fair and square!

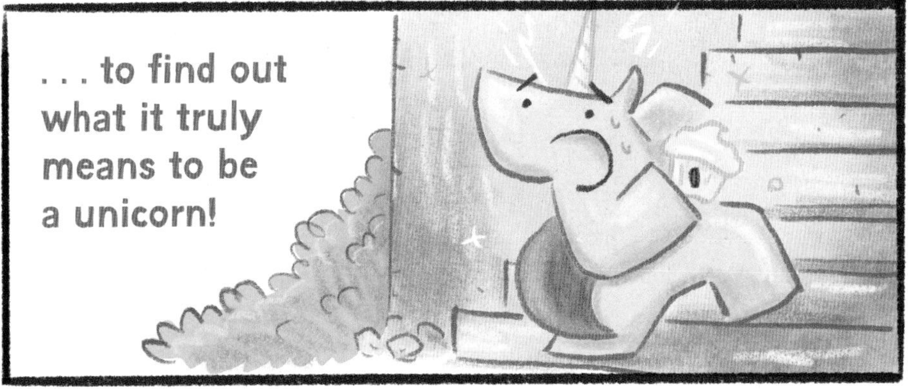
. . . to find out what it truly means to be a unicorn!

AND I'M NOT LIKE THEM!
RAHH!
CRASH!

POOF!

CHAPTER 17

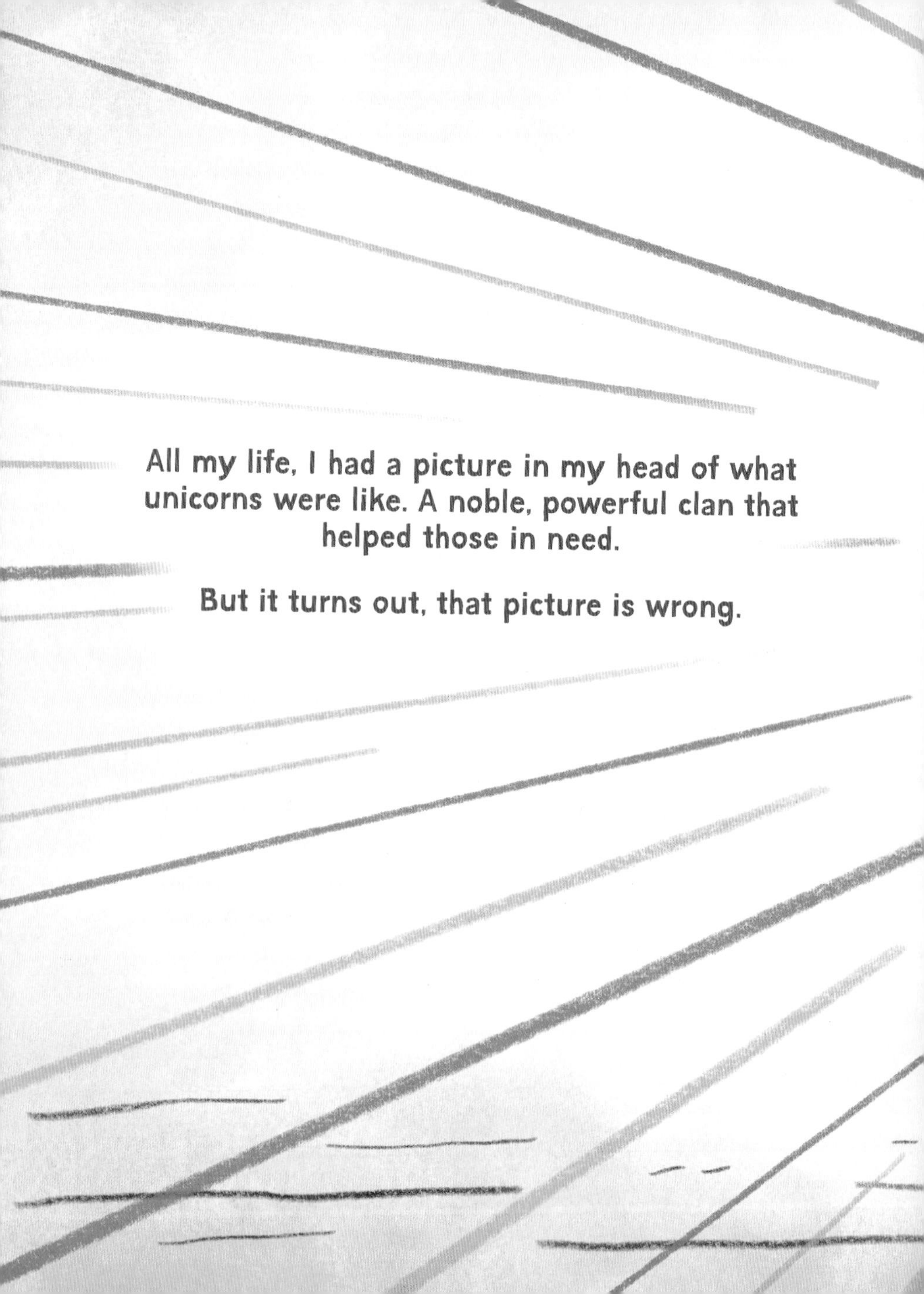
All my life, I had a picture in my head of what unicorns were like. A noble, powerful clan that helped those in need.
But it turns out, that picture is wrong.

The sparkling reputation I thought they held blinded me to the harsh truth. Like everyone, unicorns are flawed.
I plan to correct the wrongs my ancestors committed.

Aha! I knew he'd help you guys.

It's time to right the wrongs of the past.

Ooooommmm . . .
Abracadabra!
whoosh!

He's doing it.
Becoming a true unicorn.

RAH!
FOOSH!

SHOOOOOOOO!

POOF!
TA-DA!

WE'RE FINALLY FREE!

So, what are you going to do with this new freedom?

Hmmm . . . I don't know. I guess we didn't think that far ahead.

Go to the beach?
Drive one of those horseless carriages?

I don't feel so hot.

But you want to know what I'm going to do first?

herm
Oh, jeez.

Ummm. I don't know? Spit on something?
Yell at me? Take a joke too far?

WRONG!
You're yelling at
me right now.

I'm going to give you something
you REALLY deserve.
Hey! I don't want any
more trouble.

PRANKS!
A great BIG hug!
Whoa. Remember, touching me is not a good idea.
I'm so happy that I can't hear anything you're saying. Without you, we wouldn't be free.
Did he say hug?
NO! STOP!
Burp! Blerg!

BLARRRRRRGH!

This is so
embarrassing.

tick
tick

At least it tastes like cupcakes, right?

Mmm. It does!

WHY?!

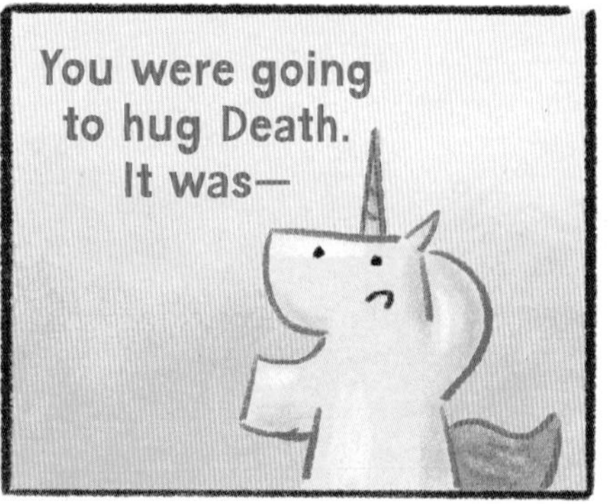

You were going to hug Death. It was—

Ohhh! Can't let anyone else have hugs, eh?

TYPICAL UNICORN! *I* need all the attention. *I* need all the hugs. And the moment you don't get what you want, you have to barf all over everyone's parade! Is this some sort of prank?

I think he just saved your life.

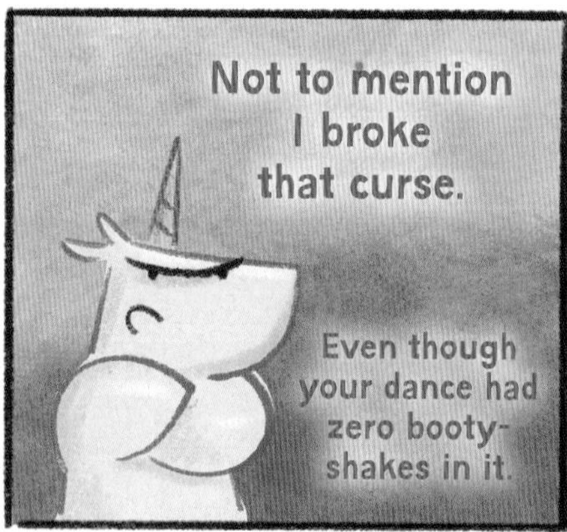

Not to mention I broke that curse.
Even though your dance had zero booty-shakes in it.

I don't care. I'll respect you, but I don't have to like you. Death, you're cool.

C'mon, gang. Let's go topside. Enjoy your stupid sacred garden.

That's enough there, Brown.
Mmm. It's so sugary.
Ptoie!

Did they just call me cool?
They must be confused.
You still want to do some karaoke?

Absolutely.

Quite the dance party, eh?
Not what I had in mind, but I feel pretty good about it.
So how did you know how to reverse the curse?
I just made up all those words. Next thing I know, spirit unicorns and smoke are exploding out of me.
Wow. That's something else. Too bad we trashed this place.
Eh. This place was long overdue for an update.
How do we get out of here?

Good
question.

What **ZANY** adventures await

DEATH & Sparkles

next?

NO!

Everyone has
to file their
own taxes!
I'm not
doing them
for you.

Please, please,
please?

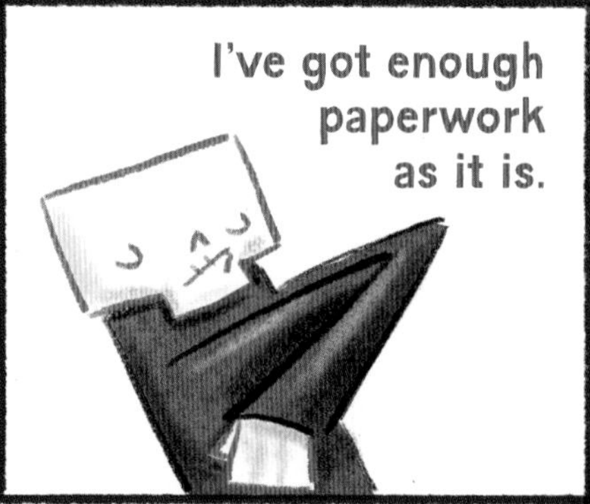
I've got enough
paperwork
as it is.

Okay. But I don't
know what to do.

Here you go.

Here's a pen.

Here's a calculator.
A calcu-what?

All right, I'm off to do some claims.

This is the worst day of my life.

YAY!
Taxes!

But what about
those surly
mole men?

THE SONNET OF SADNESS
SOLD OUT
SOLD OUT

BRAVO!
Whoo!
clap
clap
clap

Bravo! Bravo!

AH-HAHA!
Another sold-out night, my fair-footed friends.
Crunch!
(And another night of record profits!)
I've—I mean, *we've*—conquered another corner of the market:
The intellectuals!
The bourgeoisie!
The know-it-alls!
HAHA!

Okay, boys. Time to get right back out there. Still four more shows tonight.

Do we get a day off soon?

We've been working the past eleven weeks straight.

End?

ACKNOWLEDGMENTS

I started writing *Death & Sparkles and the Sacred Golden Cupcake* almost three years ago (it can take a *very* long time to write and draw a graphic novel like this). It was a very different book when I started, and it went through numerous tweaks and changes until it became this little story that I'm so proud of and that you hopefully enjoyed.

Writing this sequel was incredibly difficult for me. I placed a lot of pressure on myself to follow up the first book with something equally wacky but heartfelt. It was originally pitched as a story about ghost pirates who used to be friends with Death, then became a story about grave-robbing ghost mole men who possess Sparkles's body (yeah, I tend to start with too many ideas!), and then became what you just read. I learned a lot about writing and pushing through writer's block. I was nervous every time I submitted a revision to my editor. It wasn't until I was told that this book might be better than the first that I paused to look at all the hard work I had done through new eyes. And you know what? She was right! This is a great story and something I'm incredibly proud of (not to mention that I think the art is on point, too)!

After all the ups and downs of writing this bad boy, there are a few people I'd like to acknowledge and thank for helping me bring this series and this book to life.

First and foremost is my editor (and probably Death & Sparkles's biggest fan), Taylor Norman. You really just understood what Death & Sparkles was all about, and I could tell from our very first phone call that you just got me. You helped focus my writing on this book, and your positivity and feedback lifted my spirits more than you'll ever really know. Thank you so much for believing in these two weird characters and taking a chance on me.

A huge thank-you to my agent, Molly O'Neill, who helped take Death and Sparkles from simple one-dimensional characters and told me to build a world around them. You've helped me grow as a storyteller by leaps and bounds.

To Melissa, my beautiful partner, who always challenges me to be a better person. A better father. A better companion. A better friend. And to try and live in the moment and not worry so much about what may come. She also helped me shape Death and Sparkles into the characters that they are. Thank you for all that you do for me and our little family.

Thanks to the whole Chronicle crew for turning this series into such beautiful books for people to enjoy. Thanks, Jay, Elizabeth, Eva, Andie, Anna-Lisa, Mary, Samantha, Carrie, Mikaela, Caitlin, Claire, Lucy, Kathryn, Ashley, Kevin, Estefania, Randi, Ian, and Daria. Not to mention Fernanda at Raincoast, too (thanks for the TD Summer Reading Club hookup)!

Super hugs to those who helped develop Death & Sparkles with me. Thanks to Geoff and Amie Gibson for coming up with some of the funniest moments from book 1. Thank you to Joel Kimmel and Chantal Bennett for helping guide me through this crazy business of illustration. Thank you to Magical Weirdos—Katherine Battersby, Jo Rioux, and Alice Carter—for cheering me on and helping provide a little more heart in the series.

A super special shout-out to Hazel. You sent my first piece of fan mail, and I love all the drawings and suggestions you had for me. Thank you for helping me with my writer's block!

Lastly, thank you, thank you, thank *you* to you reading this book. I'm so lucky to have such wonderful fans. To all those I've met at talks and stores and conventions, thank you. You brighten my day and remind me why I started this journey. With that, I hope you all have bought at least three copies each and told every single person you know about Death & Sparkles to keep this series going!

High fives and fist bumps,
Robbie J.

SKETCHES
WHO Summon Me?
I feel dumb
SHH! QUIET!

I don't think I have any feet!
I think I can show you a couple steps
TA-DAH
Sparkles
Does the Muffin argument continue throughout the book?
↳ABSOLUTELY!
And to that I say:
CHEERS!
Let's see what we got here
nope nope NOPE
Oh my.
Not cool

In memory of Patrick Graham

Library of Congress Cataloging-in-Publication Data available.

ISBN 978-1-7972-0637-0 [hardcover]
ISBN 978-1-7972-0638-7 [paperback]

Manufactured in China.

Design by Jay Marvel and Kathryn Li.
Typeset in YWFT Absent Grotesque.
The illustrations in this book were rendered in magical cupcakes with a sprinkle of digital art.

10 9 8 7 6 5 4 3 2 1

Chronicle Books LLC
680 Second Street
San Francisco, California 94107

Chronicle Books—we see things differently.
Become part of our community at www.chroniclekids.com.